SKIN GROWS OVER

LUCY ELIZABETH ALLAN

Skin Grows Over

Copyright © 2022 Lucy Elizabeth Allan

First published in Great Britain 2022 by Ghost Orchid Press

This is a work of fiction. Names, characters, places, and incidents either are the product of the author's imagination or are used fictitiously. Any resemblance to actual persons, living or dead, events, or locales is entirely coincidental.

All rights reserved. No part of this production may be reproduced, stored in a retrieval system, or transmitted in any form or by any means, electronic, recording, mechanical, photocopying or otherwise without the prior written permission of the publisher and copyright owner.

ISBN (e-book): 978-1-7399968-5-7

ISBN (paperback): 978-1-7399968-4-0

Cover design © Claire L. Smith

Book formatting by Claire Saag

Dedicated to the memory of Kate Russo

1

Sometimes I think I can only feel it because I know it's there. It's more muscle memory now than anything else; my thumb finds it in that tiny crater of a scar on the heel of my right hand, catching and rolling on the fleck of stone embedded there. It looks black under the skin, or sometimes dark grey or brown like a little cancer mole, depending on the light. Some dark thing of undetermined colour, never the red it's supposed to be.

I circle it with the pad of my thumb, press and roll as it crunches softly against the insides of my hand, all the muscles and tendons that were there before it. It's an old wound now, long past hurting, but there's something left behind that's almost the same as pain; the sharpness and hardness of it, pressing into the softness of my hand, reminding me it doesn't belong inside a body.

I look down at it. I can't remember if it ever looked red once it had got stuck in there. Not bright red, not primary colour red, but red like that rust colour that autumn leaves get. Dried-blood red. I don't know how anyone who went to our primary school managed to escape red gravel embedded in their hands. Or their knees.

Ana had gravel in her knee from when Calum McCready tripped her up while she was running, so that everyone would laugh at her. She crashed onto her bare knees and elbows in the grit, but got back up and wobbled to her feet giggling, doing that odd little *ta-da* pose she used to do, like an old music hall star, and maybe it was that they were laughing at instead. But then when we were walking home together I could see her limping very slightly, both of her knees opened up and dazzlingly red. She didn't say anything the whole way home, her eyes shining with wetness just a little, her lip barely trembling.

It's got to that time of evening where it'd be dark already if it was a little later in the year. The lowering light discolours the green outside, almost into something else entirely. The colour starts to lose its cleanness. It looks older, the way bronze looks older when dirt gets into the texture of it. The green picks up brown and grey like it's grown patches of mould or damp. All the while, the wilderness gets thicker and more complex, turning into this jumble of tree trunks all twisted into the wrong shapes, and everything growing over everything else. It's all kind of a mess. It's all kind of feral.

They're ugly things, the hills outside the window. They're beautiful; on some level I know they're beautiful, but they're swollen and amorphous, growing on the earth like cysts on a scalp. Those ugly hills blend the green with brown and ochre into disjointed patches of colour. And then out of nowhere, with nowhere it could logically be coming from, this rusted, autumn-leaves, dried-blood red.

The train shudders now and then in the wilderness, where it ran smooth through the city. The train's movements have taken on that colour, now; red-tinged green. Green, tinged red.

I remember a few weeks later at school when she dug into her knee with a blade she'd unscrewed from a pencil sharpener, unflinching as the blood bloomed out from the wound then slowly began to trickle down her shin, almost reaching her ankle before she thought to wipe it away with a scratchy blue paper towel from the bathroom.

It was an operation; all of it in service of removing the dirty scrap of earth from inside her body. She became a surgeon then; her brow set, her eyes hooded and focused on the hands that were maiming her, the same expression she had when she was drawing jagged, colourful fantasy animals on the blank pages of her workbook. She did such a fine job of not showing the pain that I just assumed that she had managed not to feel it somehow, and didn't think to comfort her afterwards.

A crowd of five or six had gathered round her, and me, by the time it was finished. The blood trail she had mopped from her leg had left a red smear on her skin like smudged lipstick, and blackened the clinical blue of the now-crumpled paper towel, which she attempted to flatten out, one-handed, on the concrete bottom step at the back of the school building. Then, she scraped the corner of the bloody sharpener blade onto it. And sure enough, there in the middle of the dark stain on the paper towel, was a piece of bloody gravel the size of a sunflower seed.

She looked up at me and beamed. There was still blood dribbling out of the cut on her knee.

I became conscious after that of the smaller, subtler scrap of grit still beneath the skin of my own hand. Of the courage I lacked that might allow me to cut it out and be done with it.

It was gigantic, that red dirt pitch. Picturing it now, it stretches from horizon to horizon like some African desert. There were skeletal metal goalposts at either end, the white paint taking the metal with it as it peeled.

From one goal post to the other was too far to run. But then, I wasn't an athletic little girl. The pitch isn't there anymore; it got built over years ago, turned into council houses. I can never go back to see if it was really as big as we always thought it was. So the pitch has stayed vast and red in my memory.

I don't know the name of the stuff it was made of. I've never encountered anything like it since. That brownish, orange-red grit that stained your sandshoes, and tore up your hands and knees like a cheese grater if you fell. You'd knock handfuls of the stuff out of your shoes, and still find tiny red stones digging into your feet when you put them back on.

The movement of the train makes it feel wrong to be picturing something so still.

It was even redder in the flickering pinkish-orange of the floodlights, which would hum into being after the home-time bell rang. Right there, that image right there; that's where Ana has her flag planted. That was where we built our friendship, and where we each became certain, without ever needing to voice it out loud, that what we had built would last forever: at the sides of the pitch, sitting in the roots of the half-dead trees, our shoes stained with the gravel and our jumpers sticky with tree sap, staring out over the vast red. We were fairies, we were witches, we were cats or wolves or dragons. And the red pitch was watching us.

It watched us as we played in the roots of those trees, knowing that it had dug itself into our bodies, and that one day, long after I had watched Ana cut it out of herself, it would be under my skin to remind me of her.

I open my eyes sharply. It all goes from red to green too quickly. It makes me feel kind of sick.

It's almost dark when the train pulls into Queen Street. In the concrete of the train platform there's gum spat out and stuck so long that it's as grey and cracked as the ground. A couple of pigeons peck at nothing. None of them have all their toes: the unluckiest just has a stub of leg curled under it, useless. I used to think it was the chewing gum that did it: that the birds would step in and get stuck fast, so they couldn't even move. And their only hope of ever flying away again was to peck their foot off, or else just fly away from it, just let it tear off like a lizard's tail. I've never seen a pigeon's foot stuck to the concrete with chewing gum. I can picture it, though; it'd be curled up on itself like a dead spider.

My hand unclenches, then folds in on itself as I wait for the ticket barrier, the middle and ring finger rubbing and scratching at the fleck of grit stuck in the heel of my thumb.

I get my phone out, finally, as I walk to the bus stop. The battery's almost dead. Doesn't matter now. I bring up Ana's profile on Facebook. And there's the quickening heartbeat, the tightening of muscle in my gut, the stomach-acid burn in the centre of my chest, but it's all old news to me now. I scroll through the posts on her wall, trying to see if there's any new ones I haven't seen yet, but the kind messages have dried up. Her profile picture irritates me, because it messes with the tone of the whole page. It's the same picture it's been since Halloween last year, where she's dressed up as Daniel Day-Lewis in *Gangs of New York*, with a moustache drawn on in eyeliner, holding a plastic carving knife. I wish she'd picked something more sombre, but she couldn't have known. I wish someone could change it. I refresh it. I refresh it again. There's nothing I haven't already seen, so I read the most recent seven or eight posts, even though I almost know them by heart now.

I've walked past the bus station, I realise. I refresh the page.

There's some damage in my arm that the strap of my bag has done. It's trapped a nerve, or fucked a muscle. My arm doesn't move the way it's supposed to; it's stiff and heavy as I'm balancing the bag and trying to get the key in the door at the same time.

But there we go, we've done it, the key turns and the door clicks open and I'm home, I'm back at home and all of that other stuff is suddenly far away and ir-relevant as some foreign war on the news. I hold on tight to the wood of the door, and give my dead arm a shake so the bag slides off my shoulder and slumps to the floor, and just for a second I feel weightless. Then I can smell the scented candles that Sarah's lit and blown out, something faint and watery and almost soapy. I tug off my shoes one at a time, balancing on one foot as I lean on the door. They thump damply on the wooden floor. Half on purpose, I push the door shut too loudly, to announce my presence.

"Ali?" Sarah calls out from her bedroom, where she's left the door half-open. "You're alive! How did it go?"

I catch my own eye in the hallway mirror. I walked all the way from Queen Street without really meaning to. It only took me an hour, but the rain came on halfway through. Maybe I was too focused on my phone to realise how heavy it was getting, but right now I look like I've crawled out of the ocean. I look terrible. I look like I've been crying.

My phone is still in my hand. On the way home I found a picture of the body to show Sarah, to prove to her that I don't just sit around my room all day, and that I actually do things that are strange and interesting. But suddenly, in my flat with the door closed behind me, it looks too horrible even to look at, let alone to show Sarah. What would she think, after I showed her something like that?

The smell of her makes it down the hall a microsecond before she does. The thing about Sarah is that I would never be able to say exactly what it is that she smells like, but I know that every now and again, when I'm walking down a busy street, a girl will walk past me who smells exactly like Sarah does. I will get a waft of it, from her clothes or her scarf or her long hair. And I will always wonder if that's what a girl my age is supposed to smell like; if the ones who carry that scent are the ones who are doing it properly somehow.

"It was good, yeah. Sorry, I ended up walking back from Queen Street."

"Oh no! Is there something up with the buses?"

"No."

She's changed into her pyjamas already. She's thrown a cardigan over them, pulled tightly around herself. Her pyjamas are a matching set, a button-down top and bottoms. The cardigan kind of matches them too. Sarah has nice things; I've never been friends with anyone whose things are so nice. She dresses in a way that will carry her all the way through her twenties, probably all the way into her thirties and beyond, without it ever looking like she dresses too old or too young. Like she's already finished, and all she needs to do now is get older.

"Where was it then? If you had to get the train to get there."

I turn away from her, fussing with my bag so that she can't see me swallow the saliva in my mouth before answering. "Stirling."

Sarah's an odd one. She doesn't ask questions, and she doesn't expect me to talk about things, or get upset. It works best for both of us if there's things we just don't acknowledge. But I know she knows about Stirling, and about Ana, and I see something flash across her face right there, just as she's looking at my wet hair and the bags under my eyes. It's barely even a second, all together. If there's a discomfort in her smile for the span of that second, it's gone before I can properly register it.

"Well, good for you for going all that way for a job." She leads by example, Sarah. By smelling exactly the way she should smell, and by not pressing things. She reminds me to keep myself in check. She reminds me that just because I've brought up a picture on my phone of a dead body that's lying preserved in a museum somewhere outside of Stirling, it doesn't mean I should show anyone else.

After I've changed out of my wet clothes and deleted the picture of the bog mummy off my phone, just in case she should see it by accident, I sit down in the kitchen with her, pretending that I'm not that hungry, when actually the reason I'm only eating a bit of toast and jam is that I forgot to do my shopping again.

Sarah's getting stuff ready for tomorrow. She has seminars. "Were the people nice, anyway?"

"I don't know. They were fine." I don't know what to tell her. I hadn't even met any of them; not any of the ones I was excited to meet. I hadn't seen the bog body either, but I'd expected that. The woman who owns the museum wasn't there, the person who was going to perform the ceremony wasn't there. It was just a woman called Rebecca, who was tall and too friendly and a bit too tactile. She was one of the people who had campaigned for the ceremony to take place, and apparently she was the one who had answered my email, and decided that I should be there to see it happen in a week's time. That had made me feel kind of deflated, kind of embarrassed for reaching out. Like the decision to let me come along and shadow hadn't even come from anyone important.

"Are you going back then?"

I shrug, but don't say anything. It feels like such a waste of money now, to have gotten the bus and then the train to meet a woman who would only show me pictures of the bog body that I'd already seen, and not tell me anything about the ceremony that I didn't already know.

I hate Stirling.

"I didn't meet the celebrant, though," I say with my mouth full. That was who I wanted to meet. I wanted to see how anyone could match up to a job title like that; what kind of a person could carry off *celebrant* without a ceremonial cape and sternum-length beard. Like all those folk horror things from the seventies Ana was obsessed with for a while, where there was always this thin-faced master of ceremonies gliding about all over the place. I'd like to have seen that.

"I thought it was called an officiant," Sarah says, looking off into space for a moment while she fills her metal water bottle up from the tap. "Where did I get that from? Is there a difference?"

"Don't know." I take another bite of toast, looking at my phone. I don't look at Ana's profile, because Sarah might be looking over my shoulder. "Maybe they say officiant for weddings but not for funerals. I don't know. They usually say celebrant for funerals."

"Wait, hang on." Sarah turns off the tap, a little violently. It squeaks, that tap. "Wait, are they wanting you to do a funeral? For your first go?"

I shrug, not looking at her. "I'll basically just be watching. Just shadowing this person."

"No. They wouldn't give you a funeral to go to, would they? Not for your first day. They'd give you a wedding, wouldn't they?" She sits down in the chair opposite me, trying to fit her water bottle into her bag that's too full of uni materials for tomorrow. She looks down at my t-shirt. "That's not what you wore to see the officiant was it?"

"Hm? Oh, no, I just changed, I got rained on pretty bad. This is super old, I've had it forever."

"Let me see it?"

I lean back and pull the corners of my t-shirt out to show her what's printed on it.

"*The Wicker Man*. Is that a film?"

"You've probably seen it."

"Who's in it?"

"Christopher Lee, people like that. It's from the seventies."

She has a good look at the t-shirt, sort of making a show of being interested. She's sweet, really. She really tries with me.

"You know, I bet guys love it that you're into old movies like that. Guys always seem like they love old movies," she says, smiling at me. "I think you're on to something there."

I smile, with my mouth full.

And then she says, "I remember when all you used to do was watch films like that. When you used to just disappear into your room with your laptop and just watch films on it, remember that? As soon as you got back from lectures" She zips up her bag. "You and your friend."

The bread in my mouth mixes with seawater saliva and I have to clench my jaw tight to swallow it down. I can swallow it down. I know how to swallow it down. Because suddenly I'm there with her again: me and

21

Ana in my breezeblock room, me cross-legged on the single bed and her cross-legged on the floor, pissing ourselves laughing at *The Wicker Man*. We're first years, we're drunk on the cheapest wine we could find in Tesco; the musical numbers are hilarious, the random nudity is hilarious, the name Edward Woodward is hilarious and Ana isn't dead yet. She's in tears laughing at me laughing at Edward Woodward's name, even as Edward Woodward is being burned alive, and she isn't dead.

First years. We would have been eighteen. She'd be dead by twenty-one.

"We should do a film tonight. Shall we do that? Find something on Netflix and have a glass of wine, does that sound good?"

There's nothing I can do about it. There's nothing I'll be doing tonight but trying not to look at my phone, and ending up staring blankly at the profiles my dead friend left behind on Facebook and Twitter and Instagram and Tumblr. The worst part of herself she could have left behind for me. The part that's coldest to the touch and means the least. The part that makes me feel emptiest and loneliest and furthest from her.

That's all I do, now. It's all I do.

"I'll probably fall asleep halfway through."

"That's okay."

The mud from the walk home managed to get under my jeans and stick to my ankles. In the shower, it trickles off in little streams around my ankle bones, diluting and mixing with the water to disappear down the drain. I'm sad to see it go.

I sleep for a long, long time, my wet hair plaited and sticking to my neck. In a soft, half-awake dream, I think there is a centuries-old body lying beside me in my narrow bed, breathing quietly and smelling like earth.

I don't leave the house that week. Day and night gradually cease to be different from one another. I never ended up writing to anyone saying I wouldn't do it, that I was pulling out of the ceremony. It's too late now.

I stop caring about the mess that I'm making in my room. Things lie where I've dropped them and cover the floor; my space gradually shrinks around me until there's barely room to move. The flat has a problem with carpet bugs. I never see them, but I know they're there from the exoskeletons they leave behind when they discard them, so you know exactly where the creatures were in your room when they outgrew themselves. The abandoned exoskeletons are papery, ghostly things, as long as my fingernail, russet brown and segmented. They're brittle and delicate, and they crumble to powder when I try to flick them away without touching them any more than I have to. I find these half-powdered casings everywhere, that week.

Eventually it's the night before I go away for the weekend. For the ceremony. There's a long stretch of time where I lie awake in bed. I pull the duvet over my head and lie on my back. I tilt my head back, curl my legs into me and to the side, and let my arms extend on each side of me. It's the shape of the bog mummy in the picture. The sleeping position they found her in. I close my eyes, as if they had rotted away, and try to imagine that the sheet on top of me is a layer of cold wet dirt. I hold my breath. I try not to think anything.

I try not to think about what might be standing over my bed, watching me as I try to contort myself into its shape. It was old leather that she made me think of, when the lady in the café showed me the pictures of her; old and dried out and crackling with brittleness. But something about her made me want to picture her wet. Wet like mud, like oil.

She stands at the edge of my peripheral vision, dripping. Wet earth stains the carpet at her feet. By saying nothing, she says, you think you know about bugs?

2

I got on the first train I could after I finished work, but it still feels late by the time I get to Stirling. There's a horrible moment where I catch sight of the sky from the open-air platform, and I realise that if I don't hurry it'll be night before I get to the house. It's not the only reason I don't linger in Stirling.

I have to get a bus that seems like it's taking me miles and miles out of the city, until there's no buildings anywhere. It makes me feel lost somehow, like I've just wandered this far on my own without any means of finding my way back.

The bus leaves me at the edge of a village. When it drives off, the noise of the engine fades away into quiet and nothingness so vast I can't breathe for a second. It doesn't seem right; there's nothing here. A handful of buildings and then nothing. This isn't how the world ought to be. All I can smell is wood smoke.

I swallow the saliva in my mouth. I have the map on my phone: I check it, to make sure that this is right, that it's real, that I haven't somehow made some awful mistake and lost myself here with nothing around me and no direction to follow, and no hope of ever getting home again. I look over my shoulder at the village I've been left in, at the two or three cars and the bins outside someone's house. I can't help but feel that I've stepped outside of reality somehow, in a way that's tense and horrible, like a dream where you're sure you're about to die.

And yet the path in front of me is drawing away into the flatness and the night. That classic one-point perspective. All of it pulling back to a point in the distance like a slingshot drawn back as far as it can go. And so I just start walking. I follow the little blue line on Google Maps, and keep going. Foot in front of foot, until the last building is gone from even my peripheral vision, following that drawn-back slingshot to the point where it disappears into the night. Foot in front of foot.

When everything else is gone, this is what the Moss looks like. It's immensely flat, flat like being in the middle of the sea and being able to see right out to the curvature of the earth. Except that here, the edge of the world is marked by the outline of hills against the dark. It's treeless, wet, boggy land; brown grass and gleaming stretches of water, broken up by rough and irregular tussocks, cut through by a path made of wooden boards. And that's all there is of it, stretching out for miles in complete undisturbed silence. A bird makes a sound, here and there. There's nothing else.

This must be what astronauts feel like. I breathe in, too hard, the cold evening air stinging on the way in, maybe just to see if I still can. I can see it now, a little way out into the Moss.

I'd googled it, of course, the house that's also a museum, built on a lonely scrap of solid ground in the middle of a stretch of boggy wetlands the size of a city, where the earth is so charged and saturated with history that they cut it up and burn it like coal. I don't know how much of what's been written about it is true. From here, it looks like an ordinary cottage, squat and burly, painted white with a dark slate roof. I have to squint at it to try and pinpoint what's wrong with it. It's uneven, somehow. The symmetry's off: something grey and shapeless spilling off the side of it like a tumour. It dawns on me, in that slow, stomach-sinking way, that what's going to happen tomorrow night is going to happen here, in this house.

Do I just go up to it? Just knock on the door? I suddenly realise that it's dark already, almost as dark as it gets. I didn't notice it happening. The space is incredibly quiet, like the flatness has smoothed out the sound. Even the scattered noises of the birds become part of the silence, like the constant little noises of the human body even when it's making no sound. I'm completely exposed, completely alone. In the dark. The calmness of the fear is surprising: no panic, just a quiet, matter-of-fact awareness that I might be in horrible danger.

The path is a flimsy wooden thing, like a bridge, rotting in places and half-sunk in the bog. There's water seeping into my socks through my cheap boots, and splashing up my calves with every puddle I step in. Do people actually wander into bogs and drown, or is that just a folk tale? I start to remember something from primary school, something about creatures that hopped around in the dark with lit lanterns, luring wanderers off the paths to sink in the bog and drown. They made us close our eyes and listen to that story on a tape, made us picture them. Black-furred goblin things holding old hooked lanterns on sticks, with grins that split their faces open as they led people to their deaths. I couldn't shake it for years. I can't fucking shake it now.

There's no lights on, no movement. The wind's picked up, and gotten cold. Everything is suddenly kind of heightened, standing to attention. I can feel the beat of my heart in my neck, my arms are goosebumping under my jacket.

I don't go up to the door. I just take a minute to stand still in the middle of the flatness, because it seems like

the smart thing to do. The path has rotted away to nothing now, having led me to a solid stretch of ground
where the house stands, a little way off. I breathe in,
slowly, feel that calm, measured fear prickle my insides again. And just to make it worse, just because I
can, I take a moment to look around the vast, flat dark
of the moss.

And that's when I see the lantern.

The lurch in my gut just about knocks the breath out
of me. It's really there, so close, getting closer, a dull
blue lantern in the dark, and holding it, holding the lantern in its hand, the outline of a figure—

It's a phone. The blue light is the screen of a phone.
It's just a person, emerging from the other side of the
house, looking at their phone.

"Jesus ... " I'm breathing through clenched teeth,
trying to slow my heartbeat. I call out, "Hello?"

The person looks up. Stops. Goes still the way rab-
bits go still. She's a her. Brittle and rigid like she's
made out of wicker. I try and swallow the pulse in my
neck. The phone lights her faintly blue from below,

casting jagged shadows into the sharp peaks and valleys of her face. Her eyes are big and pale in the blue light, giving her a deer-in-the-headlights kind of look that reminds me of that thing people say about cornered animals.

"You're, uh … are you Hazel Weir? I'm Ali, I'm here, uh … for the funeral?"

The light of the phone blinks off as she puts it away, and her face fades a little further into obscurity. But I can see her, just about; whatever light that's left in the day is enough for that. She comes towards me, offers her left hand for me to shake, just as I'm instinctively holding out my right.

She smiles at me, kind of, the corners of her mouth pulling back but the rest of her face remaining fixed and stony.

"I didn't see you coming. Wasn't sure if you were going to make it before it got dark." She looks up at the night. "Was beginning to think I'd have to send out a rescue party."

"Yeah, uh ... I'm Ali, by the way. Hi." We don't end up shaking hands.

"A pleasure." She nods at my feet, "Careful where you step, by the way."

"Oh, don't worry, I've been stepping in puddles all the way here."

"No, I mean, be careful where you step."

I glance behind me at where she's gesturing and—

"*Jesus!*"

"Yeah. It's hard to see in the dark."

I turn around and back away from the massive fucking pit that looks like it's just opened up in the ground two feet behind me. I laugh, out of nowhere, at the ridiculousness of it. Hazel Weir doesn't.

"What is it?"

"I suppose it's a sort of grave. In a way," she says. Then, quietly. "You know about what's kept in there, don't you?" She cocks her head towards the house.

I nod, slowly, dumb and bug-eyed like a child.

"There's more like this one. But this is where it was taken out of the ground. She's left it here to mark the site of the whole … unburial. Or exhumation, or whatever you want to call it. Think of it as a representation of the space it left behind." She looks at me for a reaction, doesn't get one, shrugs. "Poetic, in a way. So watch your step"

Unburial. The pit is a big oblong shadow on the ground in front of me. I find that I'm hanging back on my heels as much as the waterlogged ground is letting me, as if I might need to turn and bolt at any second. I don't know why. There's nowhere I can go. I suddenly have so many questions that I have nothing to say. And the strangest part is that I should feel horrified by all of this, but somehow I can't. I don't have it in me to be scared by it.

"So, like … how deep is it?"

She shrugs, takes out her phone again and shines it into the pit. "Come see."

There's nothing else it could be but a grave. It's square cut, too deep and clean in the earth to have opened up naturally. Deeper than any grave, though; apart from those ones I read about online from long ago, graves of things deemed so terrible they had to be buried deep, with bricks in their mouths and chains around their limbs. I stand by the edge and look over. Here in the dark and the quiet it could be an opening into hell. But it smells of peat and rot instead of sulphur: an older hell, made of dirt instead of fire. Hazel doesn't come to the edge. But I almost think I see her twitching to look.

When I stand up again, she doesn't say anything. She nods at me, once, to confirm I've had my fill, stray strands of hair tossing a little in the wind, then wordlessly, she turns back towards the house. I follow. Her shoulders bob as she walks, cut to sleek corners by a good coat. I try to remember everything I read about this place, on all those shit websites with their shit believe-it-or-not clickbait articles. A couple of local think pieces about the ethical questions it raises.

My feet sink into the coarse grass, squelch and pop as they pull out of the mud. They're soaked through. Then I'm walking on stones, a rough path up to the front of the house, uneven slabs, arranged in a messy line, guiding us in. No signs or anything, nothing to suggest it's anything out of the ordinary.

She's about two feet ahead of me when she stops suddenly. I keep going, not realising, and almost collide with her. There's a jumpy little moment where I'm far too close to her. I can see her shirt collar above her coat collar, can see a little tag standing up against her neck.

She stands still at the door, as if she can't go any further. I think of vampires, stupidly, and needing permission to cross a threshold. She's looking up at the window. Even from behind her I can see that she's scanning for something from the way her head's moving. Then I see her shoulders dip as the air rushes out of her like a punctured tire.

She shakes her head. "She isn't fucking here."

"Hm? Who?"

She runs her hand through her hair, spinning to face out into the wide flat space around us. I see her jaw grind in frustration. "This is ridiculous."

Hazel glances rigidly around her, as if whoever she's waiting for is going to materialise out of the night. Her hand's still gripping her hair, her eyes are jumping around the bog. They're fucking wild.

Then she goes still. Completely still. And there's something so wrong about that that I have to physically stop myself from backing away from her. Then out of nowhere, she shouts.

"*Morag!*"

Now it's picking up. Now the panic's picking up.

"What are you doing?" She's just shouting into the night, into the expanse, as if anyone would be out there to hear her. Christ, this was a bad idea. I should never have come out here, should never had met with Rebecca in Stirling, should never have sent out that stupid email. All I wanted was something to do, something to distract me, to take me out of the city, to make me put my phone down and not think about Ana for just a little while.

"Morag!" She steps forward, away from the house, into the bog. "Morag, we had a deal!"

"Okay, stop a second, can you just … can you tell me what's going on? Stop, for just a second, okay?" I can see her face now, searching the horizon, her eyes wide and darting about.

She calls out again, her voice weaker this time. "You tell them I showed up and you didn't, alright?" There's something desperate in her face. "This is on you. Whatever trouble it gets you into, it's on you." And then she turns sharply away from me, as if she's going to stride off into the dark and disappear. She just stands there, though. Her shoulders heave slowly, just once. I wonder if she's crying. I never know what you're supposed to do when someone starts crying. I start to offer my hand towards her, not sure what I'm going to do with it.

And then she's off again, striding round to the back of the house. I immediately scurry after her, up to the door of the dark, bulging extension. God, it's kind of terrifying up close. A box of rusting corrugated metal that makes it look almost military, but with grass and weeds starting to climb up from the bottom and discolour it.

And then before I can say anything, she's grabbed the flimsy door by the handle, setting her shoulder against the wall and pulling and shaking, and Christ, you just know she's done this before, she knows exactly what to do—

I look back to at the front of the house, sure somebody's going to hear the old door rattling and clanging against its frame. "What's happening? Are we breaking into a house?" But then there's the rusty scraping sound of a flimsy lock breaking away from an unstable door frame. And the door swings open into dim space inside. Into the museum.

She cocks her head, once. *Come on.* It's not a summons. It's not an order. Just a kind of *come and see.* And I'm long past being complicit in whatever's going on. So I follow her inside.

"So wait, who were you—who's meeting us? Or, not meeting us?" I hate that I'm asking questions. I hate it.

"It's fine, we know each other. Her name's Morag Ross. She owns the house, owns the museum. Owns the guest of honour, too."

I'm kind of hanging in the doorway, slouching. "Are you sure? Are you sure this is okay?"

"We know each other. It's fine." She turns her head to look down at me. "If it makes you uncomfortable, you can go."

It's started to rain. I don't say anything. But I pull myself up a little, for her to see. A bit more angry, a bit more dignified. She thinks I'm frightened of all this.

She steps aside, courteously holding the broken door open for me to follow.

Before I knew what a funeral was, I held one, by myself, at the bottom of our little garden, in a gap between rain showers. The goldfish had died, as they're prone to do, despite me doing everything right. I had fed it and cleaned the green slime off the inside of the tank, and it had died anyway. It wasn't fair.

When it was dead, I scooped it out from where it was drifting on the top of the water, with the little green net we'd got with the tank, and I held it in my hand for a second when I knew my mum wasn't looking. It just lay there: cold and damp and clammy, exactly like the weather that day. It didn't look any different than it did when it was alive.

I laid my fish down in kitchen roll. The paper darkened with the water it absorbed from the little body. I adjusted the dead fish, just a little: fanned out the tail, brushed the fin back against its spine. There was something thrilling in the new malleability of the body. I used to dip my fingers into the tank when I was feeding it, wanting to touch it, to feel it alive under my fingers. As it lapped at the food floating on the surface, it would kiss my fingertips with its hard little mouth. But when I tried to stroke its spine, it darted away from me. Every time. It broke my little heart that my fish would only let it touch it in death. I think I cried then, because I was a child, and because it never loved me enough when it was alive to let me touch it, and because it never would now. It already smelled like decay.

I chose the spot carefully where it would be buried in the garden, under the thorns of the bramble bush. The thorns would protect it. It would be safe there. I dug a grave with my hands in the crawling dirt, flicking away the insects I dug up, because the plot needed to be sacred. I endured it all, for my fish. I didn't lurch away when a woodlouse or a centipede brushed over my hand, or even when I touched a fat wet slug, lurking like a tumour in the earth. Grief made me brave.

Ana got a couple of years into a film degree at Stirling before things got too much for her and she packed it in. One of the last times I took the train up to visit her, we got chips in the student union pub then sat there and drank until the place closed. It's in the middle of nowhere, that uni. Hills, forest, loch, on all sides. So when we got kicked out of the union and our faces hurt from laughing at nothing, we were kicked out suddenly into the wilderness.

And I don't know how to accurately remember this, looking back; maybe it's just because we were so completely fucked from the £2 pints, but going from a cramped space full of people and pool tables and TV screens showing music videos from ten years ago, and stepping out into the night air to find nothing but the vast quiet dark of that wild campus waiting for us, that did something to us that day. I can't explain it. You just breathe in and the world isn't what you thought it was.

We walked along beside the loch, with one of the university buildings next to us. Ana's hair was still down to her shoulders, then. She wore tattered Converse despite the rain, and I could see them getting more and more soaked through as I watched her steps instead of mine. Her feet squelched in the grass. She was gesturing as she talked, the way she did when she was drunk: jagged, rhythmic hand movements like some shit rapper, using up all the space around her, because what we were saying was that important. I don't remember what we were talking about, but it was profound and heartbreakingly sad, and beautiful, and so funny it winded me like a punch in the chest. I couldn't tell if it was me talking, or her, or it was neither of us and we were communicating just by thinking into each other's brains. It was like we were the same person.

Then there was a crack like a gunshot as some dark something flicked across the path in front of us and was gone. Ana grabbed my hand, stopped in her tracks and stopped me with her. There was a blackbird, dead by the side of the path. Its wings splayed out, its head turned to one side. No wounds, no sign of harm; it had flown into a window that had reflected the night like a mirror, and died instantly.

Neither of us spoke, staring at the blackbird. We were still for a moment, in the dull reddish glow from the streetlights that lit the loch at night. We didn't discuss what we did. We couldn't see the colours of the leaves and scattered flowers in the dark, but we collected them anyway. Twigs and damp leaves as well, handfuls of grass. We made a nest for it. A protective circle around the bird like the one it was born in. It was thorny, unruly, safe. We scattered the flowers over its body, over the nest, like a blessing.

We looked at it for a long time once we had finished. We wanted to carve our initials into the tree above it but we didn't have anything sharp. I remember thinking, later on, it was a good thing we didn't. That would have made it look like we were in love.

I didn't go to Ana's funeral. I couldn't bear to see it for myself. I thought I would stay in bed crying all day, but I didn't. I cried myself out within half an hour, then ran out of tears and had the whole rest of the day to fill somehow. I spent it in a haze; fogged up like a car window. I sat for the whole day watching American sitcoms on my mum's Netflix account, and feeling absolutely nothing.

3

It's dark inside. Hazel hits a switch and the light comes on, kind of. It's a weak, strained light that hums and pulses and doesn't illuminate the space so much as colour it, casting a dull orange glow over the middle of the room. I look up: strip lights, like in a warehouse. If I didn't know what was in it, the whole place would seem like a warehouse: a bleak, empty space, the size of it difficult to guess, with the far corners of the room still in almost total darkness. It feels somehow colder than outside, like the wind is blowing straight through the walls, something a little musical in the sound of it battering the thin metal.

"Here she is," Hazel says, softly. "This is our guest of honour."

She moves aside, giving me space to look. In the centre of the room is a long oblong shape, covered in a silky, dark-coloured sheet. A veil, you'd probably call it, given the context. The corners of the box are sharp underneath. I just know there's a glass box under there. There's a little light shining on it from a cobwebby window in the slanted ceiling. I'm going to meet her in person.

The picture I'd found to show Sarah swims into my brain again with such clarity, it's almost like she's here standing behind me, itching to see herself laid out like a queen, craning over my shoulder to get a better view. I almost think I feel breath on the nape of my neck.

I look back at Hazel, for reassurance, guidance; I'm not really sure what. But she isn't looking, she's staring at the veiled box, looking like she's not quite here, one hand held to her chest, fingers twitching distractedly. I can see her better, in the orange half-light, coloured in by the fading bulb. Not much better, but better enough. She's kind of hard to look away from once you start: the raised bridge of her nose, and her hooded eyes; the kind of light brown that seems to have a little yellow in it. Just a bit hawkish.

"Can I look?" I ask. This focuses her: she runs her hand over her hair, pushing it back out of her face—it's coarse and dark and tied loosely in a knot at the base of her skull. A few strands curl around the lobes of her ears. She has a strange coarseness to her, I think. Like raw silk. Then she nods, with a grimness I wasn't expecting.

"Look, it's an exhibition, that's what she's here for." She sees me hesitate, softens a little. "There's a lot of people who don't think it's ethical, you know that already. You can make up your own mind about that side of it all. But you wouldn't be the first person to be disgusted that she's being kept in here."

I almost don't want to see, now I'm here. Almost. "Does that include you?"

"Does what include me?"

"Are you disgusted by it?"

She looks surprised that I asked her. She takes a second to consider this, her mouth slightly open, waiting for the right answer to come. Then she shrugs.

"I understand the appeal of it. It isn't anything that hasn't existed before. In Victorian times people used to pay to go see doctors cutting up corpses, did you know that? Whole towns turned out to see public hangings, once upon a time. If that really is built into human nature, if there's a part of us that really does want to see other human beings unmade, I suppose someone has to sell us a corpse."

I look back to the veiled coffin. But I think I saw a change in her, there. Just a hint of delight. A dark, secret kind of delight just visible below the surface, like the orange glint of a fish in a murky pond.

I kind of feel like I shouldn't look, now. I do anyway. I've come all this way to see a dead person. I'd have paid to see a corpse get cut up if I was a Victorian. I'd probably have been first in line. I imagine the body still standing at my shoulder, starting to get excited now.

I lift a corner of the veil on the coffin podium. Just a little —just enough to look inside. Doesn't seem right to whip the whole thing off like I'm unveiling a sports car. I have to crouch to see what's underneath.

"Is there another light you can turn on?" I don't expect her to do anything, but I hear her footsteps come towards me as I'm staring into the black glass of the box, and the next thing I know she's knelt down beside me, her arm against my arm. She takes out her phone and shines the harsh blue light into the glass coffin.

I squint past the glare and the reflection, lift the veil a little higher to see what's inside.

"Fuck."

There's a farmhouse door leading from the museum into the house itself. It's unlocked. Hazel doesn't have to break it open.

The wind has picked up outside. Really picked up: I can hear it whistling and whining the way you can only hear it when you're in a house that's old and frail in the middle of nowhere. You can hear the flatness of the land in the wind; there's nothing here to slow it down. The rain is starting to drum against the windows, too. It's warm and calm in the living room. That adds to the strangeness as well: this disconnect between the outside world and this separate, sheltered one.

The room smells damp and a little stale, only slightly less peaty than the outside. I like the carpet: it's a deep red, patterned with yellow-brown fleur-de-lis, breaking up the dark shapes of stains as best it can. The wood of the furniture, the low beams and the cornicing is all the same, reddish and worn, framing the small space in a strange wooden skeleton. Kind of feels like being inside something's belly.

We sit slumped, tired like the last two old men in a pub. She seems at home in the quiet where I'm not, drumming noiselessly on her knee with one hand. I hold on tightly to the arms of my chair to stop myself fidgeting. We sit opposite each other on two armchairs in the bright centre of the big, dusty room, under a pendant light with a weird stained-glass shade. There's something about it that feels exposed and claustrophobic at the same time. My rucksack with my pyjamas and toothbrush is lying at my feet. I don't know how I'm going to sleep here tonight.

"You ever seen something like that before?"

I shake my head. "No. I mean, I saw pictures online. I did some research on this place, and there were pictures. But no, not … in person."

"Do you know much about her?"

"Who, this Morag person? No, I mean, I only heard you talking about her—"

A flick of a smile. "No, that's not who I mean." She nudges her head towards the farmhouse door separating us from the museum. Her. It had been a her.

"Oh … " My mannerisms have gone all weird and out of character. I'm holding my hands together now, pressed palm-to-palm between my knees. "Only what I've read online. Should I … do you think I should know more about her? Like, before it all happens?"

She looks at me, her pupils swollen and black in the dim room, holding on to the eye contact for longer than is comfortable. Then she looks away, with a half-hearted little smile that crinkles the skin at the corners of her mouth.

"Rebecca told me you're looking into becoming a celebrant."

For a moment, I can't think who Rebecca is, then I remember that was the name of the woman who met me in Stirling.

"Yeah, I don't know. Thinking about it."

"I should have gotten back to you myself. I'm not great with answering emails. Sorry about that."

"Oh." I wasn't expecting an apology. "That's okay. Is it your wi-fi or something?"

She shakes her head. "I just really don't enjoy typing. It's very slow and tedious for me." Her eyes flick away as she holds up her right hand for me to see. It's oddly limp. Rigid. "This hand doesn't really work any more. Not for some time now. Long story."

"Fuck. Sorry, I mean … sorry about that."

She shrugs. "They think she might be a thousand years old, did you know that? A thousand years in the ground." She pulls her faulty right hand into herself a little, as if to stop me looking at it. Which obviously makes me notice it more. "It's not a real funeral. It's just a blessing. To acknowledge that she was a person once, not just a thing. That's what Morag agreed to. It's … " she gestures vaguely with her one working hand, "it's something, you know? At least it's something."

"And they couldn't have gotten a priest or someone to do it? Someone local?" I yawn, suddenly, almost before I've finished talking. I'm tired already. I run my hands over my face, rubbing my fingers into my eyes, massaging bursts of coloured light into my field of vision. I look down at my fingers and they're smeared in mascara. "*Shit.*" I forgot I had makeup on.

Her eyes are on me again, which I don't like. Reminds me of how cats stare you right in the eye when they're about to bolt away out of nowhere. There's a silence. Her hands, one broken, one functioning, are gently resting on the carved armrests of her chair. She's sitting back, but not slouching. She looks like a votive statue.

"It was Morag's call. She owns the body on a technicality; it was dug up on land that she owned. And she stood her ground and fought against any sort of ceremony being performed for years and years, all because she didn't want anything religious touching it." Her hand and her eyebrows twitch in unison. "It's ... she has a thing about that. But Rebecca and her friends kept pushing, until eventually Morag caved and agreed for a humanist ceremony to be performed. As long as it was nonreligious, and as long as it was performed by me."

I look up and she's watching her own hands like she isn't quite sure what they're going to do next. How do you lose the use of an entire hand? Would it have been an injury, an illness? I slump further into the armchair and pick at the stone in my own hand. The chair's too old to be comfortable. I can feel a lot of springs.

I want to ask her about the bog body, but I don't know what it is I want to know; I could ask about how she died, what her life would have been like, how old she would have been. But I want to know more than that; I want to know what kind of effect the body has on people, if it's normal that I can't seem to stop thinking about her. I want to tell her that more than once this week, when I've been trying not to think about anything and I've let my eyes lose focus, I'm sure it's the shape of the bog mummy I've seen skulking at the edge of my vision.

Hazel's looking up at the clock on the wall, clearly still annoyed at Morag's absence, while her hand, the working one, plays with a strand of hair that's come loose from her untidy bun.

"So how long have you been doing the whole humanism thing?"

She looks at me, still stroking her hair absentmindedly.

"Like, the celebrant thing. How long've you been a celebrant? 'Cause I am interested. You know, potentially."

She tips her head sideways to think. "Officially? I don't know, maybe three years now. Unofficially, a lot longer. But that's another story."

"Unofficially?"

"It's not really worth getting into."

"And you make a living doing this, do you? You get a lot of work? Cause from what Rebecca told me about you, it seems like you're kind of … niche."

She shrugs. "People like niche. Niche means specialised." She folds her arms behind her head and stretches, pushing her chest out in front of her. It's mastectomy flat. Then she stands up and wanders over to the clock, circling her shoulder back like there's a crick in it she can't stretch out.

"'Cause it's just funerals you do, isn't it?"

"Funerals for women," she says. "Exclusively women, exclusively funerals." She stops pacing, looks up at the clock. In profile, her cheekbone curves inward like a question mark. The collar of her coat underlines the sharp cut of her jaw. A good face for her line of work. She looks down at me. "So what, is this why you contacted me? Are you wanting me to give you advice? You want me to tell you how to do this job, is that why you're here?"

"I honestly don't know why I'm here. But, like ... sure."

"Okay." And she looks me in the eye this time. I see something flicker in her face then, glinting like a knife edge catching the light, and then gone so quickly it might never have been there at all.

She holds up one finger. "First thing. Your instinct will be to make yourself as open and personable as you can be for your clients. Ignore that instinct. Display a reasonable amount of empathy and understanding, but don't try and be their friend. They don't want that. The minute you let them make tea for you or ask about their families, you've broken a boundary. You've over-lapped your world and theirs. Because you're coming into their homes not quite as a representative of death, but as something like a translator for it. An envoy. Never forget that. People don't want death to be nor-mal: you are something that people need to distance themselves from. So be distant."

She holds up another finger. "Second thing, you need to write services, so get good at writing. People go to a funeral, they want the story of a person. You are fictionalising someone's life, so make it worth telling. Doesn't matter how peaceful or uneventful their lives might have been; milk the survivors for every fact and every detail. Extrapolate everything. Pull the imagery out of it. So the dead woman's done nothing but live in the same house and work the same job all her life. You can turn that into anything. Steadfastness, loyalty, perseverance, peacefulness. Everything's a metaphor for anything. There is a language of symbolism that is as natural to us as breathing; you already understand it, you just need to learn to speak it. You can shape a life into anything you want it to be."

She looks at me again, more searchingly this time, those pupils still swollen and black. "Why do you want to be a celebrant?"

"I don't know," I tell her. Which isn't entirely true. Her eyebrows knit together a little. Those hooded hawk eyes don't move from mine, like she's waiting for me to say more. And I suddenly get the feeling that if there's ever going to be a right moment to ask her about the bog body, it's right now.

There's a loud clatter from the museum room. A screech and rattle of a broken metal door being wrenched open again. The wind's been let into the house: it rushes under the closed door to the living room and I get a shock of cold. And it's the bog mummy I think of; I can't help it. I think of her slipping out of her coffin, climbing unsteadily to her feet, ambling blindly towards us, her hands stretched in front of her.

There's a second where Hazel goes rigid like a pointer, like her ears would be pricked up if they could. I almost think she might be thinking the same thing as me. Then, I don't know if it's the shuffling of feet, or the sound of a chair being dragged clumsily back into an upright position, but she's at ease again. I'm not.

Instead of opening the door she stands like a doorman, waiting patiently for whatever she's expecting to come through. I've gotten up from the chair without noticing. I might have jumped. I'm watching her watching the door, expecting some stranger or the wind to come rushing through at any moment.

Then she turns to me, unexpectedly, her face softer than before, almost kind. It's the softness that jars. There's still clattering coming from behind the door. I almost don't hear her when she speaks.

"Look, there's … there's another thing you should know about the symbolism of it all. And you're going to think this is stupid, but it's something I wish I'd been told at the beginning. People are going to resent that you're a woman. Death happens to us. We're its victims: we die and other people are sad about it. We don't stand next to death and help others comprehend it. They won't let it show, they won't say anything to your face, but to them, you are an affront. So, y'know … don't take it personally."

She gives me a twitch of a smile that doesn't extend to the rest of her face. She turns back to the door and it's gone. She fixes the collar of her coat. "Death enacts violence on us. We bear that suffering, in silence if we can, and we don't try and gain power over it."

The door is pulled open from the other side. The wind swoops in, cold and fresh.

"You broke my fucking door, Weir!"

Morag Ross knocks the breath out of the room the second she steps in. The air seems to rush into her all at once, and all at once the space resettles itself around her. She's in her sixties: fat, weather-beaten and ruddy-faced, and kind of beautiful for it. The orange-brown dye in her hair starts a few inches from her centre parting, where there's a badger stripe of gunmetal grey. She pulls off her big puffy workman's coat with an *oof* and an audible crack somewhere in her body. She heaves and creaks like an old ship.

"Broke my bloody door," she says, not quite under her breath, swaggering, noisily and almost aggressively over to Hazel. But all she does is gently, warmly squeeze the top of her arm, and something casual and effortless gets passed between them, and I get it now.

She only agreed to the ceremony on the grounds that it was Hazel doing it. There's an old and solid thing between the two of them that goes deeper than timekeeping and broken doors. I feel very lonely, out of nowhere.

"And this must be the protégée," she says, taking my hand in both of hers and gripping so tightly I think she might be able to feel the stone there. Her hands are sweaty and hot. "Morag. Lovely to meet you, pet. It's Alison, isn't it?"

"Yeah, Ali." And then, because I feel like I should be saying something else, "Your friend's shown me the dead person already."

She winks at me with gambler's sleaze, and grins, showing a row of squat little teeth and a lot of gum. "I bet she has, darlin'. I bet she has."

She puffs herself up and stands up straight so she's almost my height, and claps her hands onto my shoulders. I almost lurch away at the sudden physical contact, at the forwardness of it. But then she turns me, gently, by my shoulders, so that Hazel is gone from my peripheral vision. Just me and her. I have the intense, unfamiliar feeling of being looked at, close-up: not judged, just seen.

"Didn't know if you'd show up, petal," she says quietly, hoarsely, in a low crunch of a voice. "But I shouldn't have doubted you, I see that now. You just wanted to get a look at her for yourself, didn't you? You're a watcher. You're a listener. I can see it in your face." She reaches out to stroke my cheek and doesn't take her fingers away when I flinch at the touch. "You know how I can tell? 'Cause of where the wrinkles are." And she runs one finger along the shadows under my eyes, and up to the crease between my eyebrows. "Aye, you're dead young still, but they're coming, They're on their way." Then she tuts. "Ach, bless you, come here." She licks the pad of her thumb and rubs under my eye where I smudged my mascara.

I can smell the rain on her.

"I could understand people being upset if I made money off her; that, I could understand. And I've made it clear many a time, that I don't charge admission. She's here, she has the gallery space to herself, and if people want to come in and see her, they can. And if they want to leave a small donation as well, I'm happy with that. But they can't be upset about her being in here, not after all this time."

I've never seen two people who occupy space so differently from one another. Hazel moves to the edges of things, hugging the walls, staying calm and still, apart from her eyes which roam about everywhere, sometimes landing on mine and staying there for a second, before flicking away.

Morag stands in the middle of the room and fills up the space like sand in a bucket.

"She's a local legend. She's made it onto Atlas Obscura, Ali, have you heard of that?"

"Yeah. I saw that."

"And listen, as long as I get to keep her, I can make peace with whatever happens today. Better this lot getting their way than the Church that wants a good Christian funeral for her. I've been fending that attention off for nigh on thirty years now. They want her blessed and buried; they want to take her away from me and put her back in the earth. Better it's a bunch of local hippies who just want the ceremony of it all."

She turns to Hazel. Again, that unexpected warmth in her voice. "Sorry, petal, you'll be bored of all this by now."

I see Hazel smiling back: very subtly, in the crinkle of her eyes. "We waited up for you, Morag." She glances over to me as if expecting me to back her up. "We didn't know if you were going to show face."

Morag nods, a little grimly. "Aye. I was just doing the rounds, pet. You know how it is. Just needed to see to things." She exchanges a look with Hazel that isn't for me to understand. There's something stern and almost chastising in Hazel's expression, something almost childlike in Morag's. Then it's over, whatever it is, and Morag turns back to me.

"I'm keeping you from your bed, now, pet," she says. Giving my shoulder a squeeze. "Should have been here, shouldn't I? When Hazel brought you to see her. Should have helped introduce the two of you. Never mind. You'll get to know each other well enough tomorrow."

She doesn't know, of course, how well acquainted I already am with the bog body. I get a shiver, out of nowhere. It's cold in here, after all; it seems like the night time has sucked the warmth out of everything, or like the ground is too soggy and soft to hold heat.

"Right!" says Morag, clapping her hands with such a force that I can see her upper arms jiggle though her fleece. "Bedtime. Let's get ourselves good and rested up for tomorrow. It's going to be a weird one." I see that this gets a flicker of a smile from Hazel as she slips out of the room, not staying for the goodnights.

I hold my rucksack close to me as I follow her, completely outside of myself, politely telling Morag to sleep well as I go.

She winks at me again. "Don't be having bad dreams, now."

4

Night hits you differently in a place like this one; it takes you out of the world entirely and puts you down somewhere else, somewhere that doesn't seem like it's got a beginning or an end, and where silence just about takes on a new meaning, like you've never truly been in the quiet before. Anything that breaks that silence makes you panic for a second, like your brain's devolved to something a bit primal, that has to be constantly listening for danger.

The museum space is very big when you're standing in it alone. It feels like an empty factory floor; looking up I can see the bare rigging of the strip lights and the skeleton of the roof. It's cold. It feels like there's a wind blowing through the room, even though it's the sound of the battering wind outside, and I'm safe from it in here. It feels exposed the same way a mountain top might feel exposed. She shouldn't be in here.

Morag didn't lock the door to the museum room. I was coming back from the bathroom to the sofa that had been made up as my bed in a spare room, when I'd stopped and tried the handle, not expecting it to open. And once the handle had turned in my hand, it felt like it wasn't even my choice whether to go in or not.

The body looks like a leather glove once the hand's been taken out of it; empty and ghostly, just about keeping the shape of the thing it used to hold. Her skin's stained all dark; that rich, peaty colour that old whisky is supposed to have. Bits of pale hair wisp over her face. Her features are shrink-wrapped in too-tight skin; there's deep folds where it's pulled back from her mouth and eyes.

Except that she doesn't have eyes any more: you can tell by the way her eyelids are wrinkled up and shrunken in on themselves. Her lips are pulled back; grimacing like she's gritting her teeth through some unimaginable pain. Teeth are still there. That's something. She's laid out on her side, curved into herself like a question mark; I follow the gaunt hook-shape of her body to her limbs. They seem to wither and shrivel up as they go, as if she's slowly being unravelled from her hands and feet upwards.

She's old leather. She's tough, dried-up meat. I glance back up to her face again, guiltily. No reaction. Then I let the sheet fall back over the glass coffin, and smooth it out so that it lies flat with no wrinkles, as if I'm tucking her in.

The other version of her, the version that I've now accepted will be following me around for the time being, watches me do all this with an expression that's inscrutable. She's stock still, but oddly tense, like she wants to intervene or speak up on her own behalf, but doesn't quite have the energy. Maybe she seems more slumped than she did previously. She's tired. Her movements, when she tags behind me to leave the empty, echoey space of the museum room, are all sluggish and inelegant like something that was never human in the first place. It's an effort for her, I think, being a person.

It's only then that it occurs to me to wonder what she makes of all this; what she makes of me coming up here and messing with her resting place. What she makes of being pulled around after me. The house is very dark, and very old, and it creaks and murmurs at uncomfortable times. What I don't want to do is look behind me and see that withered, skeletal figure loping after me in the dark, and feel that it resents me.

A movement along the hallway makes me jump.

"Oh god, I didn't see you there, pet!" Morag screeches a laugh that makes me flinch slightly. Hazel is sleeping here tonight, too. I'm conscious of her presence in the house.

"Christ, I need to start turning lights on in this bloody hall. How are you doing, my love, is everything comfortable?" A light comes on. She's wearing a dressing gown that smells like it hasn't been washed in a while. It's pale blue, patterned with pastel-coloured stars, like something that a child would wear. Her feet are half-hanging out of slipper socks with a white fleecy lining and those little beads that stop your feet from slipping. Her heels are rugged and cracked. She hardly lifts her feet as she shuffles towards me, bent ever so slightly over to one side, her whole body seeming to heave as she breathes. I suddenly feel very small next to her.

"Have you got everything you need with you? Pyjamas, all of that? I can give you a loan of anything you've forgotten, just so's you know. Course, you'll drown in anything that's mine, but don't let that stop you asking. You can have a t-shirt to wear as a nightie if you like, no problem at all."

"I've got an overnight bag. Thank you, though."

Morag puts her hands on her hips and looks back over her shoulder at the living room, puffing out her cheeks slightly. Her breathing is loud and raggedy. She looks rough; her hair sticks out from her head, knotted in big tangles. There's something else—it's half-dry, like she's been in the shower. Or out in the rain.

"You want a cup of tea in the front room before you go to bed? I might have one. I've got some fancy teas in there; herbal ones, the kind that won't keep you up." She rubs the back of her hand over her eyes. I wonder suddenly if she's been crying. Her face is puffy, swollen, but gaunt at the eyes like she hasn't slept in days.

I open my mouth to say something, but I'm not sure what it is I want to say. I look over her shoulder towards the living room, trying to imagine myself as the kind of person who could sit up with a cup of tea and get to know somebody like that. "I just … I'm kind of tired."

She nods, enthusiastically. "'Course. 'Course, you've come all the way here. It's been a long day for you, hasn't it? Alright love, you'll get a good night's sleep on my sofa. I've put a lot of friends up in there, it makes a good wee bed."

When she smiles again, there's something a little embarrassed in her expression. With a little huff, she leans against the wall with one arm, taking one of her feet in the other hand, rubbing. "Do you know, Ali, I feel a bit guilty that I asked you to come tonight instead of tomorrow morning. That's alright, isn't it? It's alright that I'm making you stay over tonight?"

I'm genuinely surprised by the question. She catches my expression and puffs out a laugh.

"Yeah, I say. Yeah, genuinely, it's fine. It makes total sense, I had to come up from Glasgow."

She lets go of her foot and thumps me warmly on the arm, still leaning against the wall. "Oh, thank god. God, I just ... I didn't want you to feel scared or uncomfortable, or like you couldn't relax or, I don't know, like I was going to murder you in your sleep. It's surreal enough having to stay in a strange old lady's house at the best of times, I appreciate that, but—"

"It's genuinely—it's fine."

She holds up a finger to stop me, not impolitely. "*But*," she continues, "I wanted you to see her. Before people arrive tomorrow morning; I wanted you to see her and get to ... " she waves her free hand as she searches for the right words, " ... get a sense of her. Of what it feels like to be in a room with her. You understand that, don't you? I wanted to give the two of you some space."

And then she winces and half-bends to rub her foot again. I'm very aware that I'm standing doing nothing while she's clearly in pain.

"Are you … is everything alright? Can I do something?"

"You can make yourself at home, pet, and get yourself rested up for tomorrow." For a second, her face contorts in pain. She rattles out a sigh that reminds me of the heating coming on in an old house. "It's, uh … It's going to be a weird one."

I look over her shoulder down the hall, not wanting to look her in the eye. There's a pair of wellies lying by the door where they've been kicked off, caked in mud.

I don't know how to ask this. "Is it okay that I'm here? That I'm staying here, that I came to shadow Hazel? I know it wasn't, like … your idea."

She scoffs. "Alison, pet, none of this was my idea," she gives me a very sad, very genuine smile. "You being here is the nice bit. I mean that."

There's a moment where I think she wants me to hug her. But I don't. She pats me on the shoulder, and then, as she huffs past me down the corridor, she calls out, "Watch your step in the hall, pet! I've left stuff lying around. Couldn't be bothered tidying it away."

Then she's gone.

I look down. And for some reason, what's lying at my feet makes my heart stutter in something very close to horror. There's a spade lying in the doorway between the hallway and the kitchen. A massive, industrial-sized spade, the kind that I've had no reason to see up close before, only at a distance in parks or the grounds of my old school.

The blade of it is massive; so big it throws the whole thing off balance, stuck on the end of the wooden shaft like a head on a pike. It's covered in mud, dripping with it; there's fresh bog scattered all over the faded linoleum. There's flecks of bracken in the mess. I hurry back to my room like I've just witnessed a crime.

That night, huddled against the cold on an old sofa, is the first night where I don't think about the bog mummy as I drift off to sleep. For some reason, I'm thinking of the pit in the earth that Hazel showed me. That perfect oblong, cut into the turf. I'm thinking about the word *unburial*.

It was repulsion, in the end, that made me realise that it was time to cut ties with Ana for good, five months before she died. The disgust response, when it's strong enough, brings something like fear with it; like there's a chance that whatever it is you're repulsed by might touch you somehow, that it might infect you, or corrupt you.

She had been a problem for me for a long time before that, but I always found a way to explain to my new friends why she dressed like that, and talked the way she did, and I learned to do it with enough of a smirk or an eye roll to show that whatever she was doing was her thing and not mine; that I wasn't connected to it.

Her openness and the way she spoke became an issue for me after spending a long enough time at a distance from it. The things she said started to turn gross and ugly. Or they had always been gross and ugly, and I was only just waking up to it.

I went with her to a gig at some strange and kitschy little place tucked away round the corner from the big Odeon I used to work in, all neon-lit and decked out like the old west. The Grand Ole Opry, that was what it was called. It was someone Ana liked, some androgynous young woman with a guitar, singing the kind of songs that I'd only ever heard old men sing before. I dipped in and out of drunkenness and sobriety all through that evening. When I'd gone for too long between drinks and the alcohol was losing its effect, I became embarrassed and self-conscious, and unable to take my mind off what I would say if someone I knew from uni saw me here. When the drinks were working, and I was drunk enough to hold Ana's hand, I thought

this woman's songs were the most beautiful things I'd
ever heard.

I was dead sober when we walked across the river
to the train station. More sober than I wanted to be.

She told me about the skin on her nipples, out of
nowhere, when we were walking together across the
bridge— the one that lights up purple when it's dark
and swoops across itself in a big white arc—when there
was no one else around she could have told me about
anything in the world. The purple light from the bridge
reflected in the water.

She told me that once her eczema got so bad that the
skin on her nipples had dried up, so much so that one
day they had both just cracked open. The skin had split
apart, exposing something underneath that was hot
pink and angry, that stuck to the inside of her bra and
had to be peeled away from it at the end of every day.
Something that refused to close up.

Then, when I couldn't think of anything to say to
that, and we'd spent a moment just walking across the
bridge in silence, she said, "I have this theory that I

kind of manifested that somehow. That I projected so much of what I hate about having this body onto my tits that they started to rot apart like damp wood." There was a silence. "I don't want them to rot away. I don't want anything to happen to them. I just wish I'd never had them in the first place."

And all I could think of was the red insides of her knees that day in primary school, and now I felt like I had seen the angry, hot pink flesh inside her breasts. And that I had never asked to be invited inside her.

I felt disgust, then. But it was more than that; it came with a sort of fear that I might be the same as she was somehow, beneath the skin. That was the real fear; if I started to crack apart as well one day, and found that I had something hot pink and angry on the inside of me, just like she did.

The house, first thing in the morning, is very cold. There's a moment just after I wake up from the sun through the window where I have no idea where I am. And then I lie in the cold, a blanket huddled around me and the sunlight in my eyes, letting it all come back to me, in a state that feels genuinely otherworldly.

She's in my room again. Not doing anything. Just standing there. Just watching. I get dressed quietly, turned away from her and with a blanket slung round my shoulders, so that she doesn't see anything.

Every floorboard, every hinge of every door in this house makes a noise. I know that I won't have the gall to make coffee or go looking for breakfast in a stranger's house, but I go towards the kitchen anyway, because it seems like the best place for Morag or Hazel to find me fully dressed and ready for the day.

But as I make my way down the hall, I see that the door leading to the museum room is open again. I hesitate outside it for a moment, and suddenly the reality of what I'm supposed to be doing here today comes very close to bursting out and overwhelming me. For some reason it is now, in the daylight, separated from the displayed body by a sturdy half-open door, that the strangeness of it all seems most threatening.

I can sense the bog mummy at my side again. I try to stop myself from shrinking away from her, and instead try my best to ignore her, and move closer to the door as if she wasn't here. I suddenly don't like the idea of her hovering around me for the rest of the day. After all this time, I still haven't quite been able to identify what kind of presence she is. I get the sense of a twitchy, impatient movement in my peripheral vision. I worry that if I try and forget she's there altogether, or try and banish her some other way, she'll come back a darker thing, full of malice at having been forgotten. And what happens when all this is over? When I go back home, back to my life, do I really think she's just going to stay behind?

I swallow, even though my mouth is dry, and look through the open door. I don't know who I expect to see there; I know it wasn't me who left the door open last night, so really it could only be one of two people.

But it's still a shock to see Hazel there, standing soldier-straight by the veiled glass coffin.

The catch in my breath doesn't make a noise, so I stay there, watching her without her realising, until I can get a grasp of what she's doing. She's standing with a hand resting on the glass of the coffin like a mother with a premature baby in an incubator. She's got a little spotlight on her from where the morning is coming through the rusted-shut skylight. Her lips are moving. Then she moves her hands so that they're clasped together, still resting on the glass of the veiled glass. Her head sinks into a bow.

I don't breathe. I want to hear what she's saying, but she's too far away. And then, as if sensing my presence, as if she's been notified by whatever god she's praying to, she looks over her shoulder, right at me. I lurch away from the door, and slip down the corridor to lock myself in the bathroom.

By the time I've showered and changed back into my clothes, the congregation has arrived. The front door has been left open and the sunlight and the sound of people comes down the hall like a cold draught. I haven't seen Morag this morning; if she's not here, or not awake yet, it means I'll have to greet these people myself. Not just that, I'll have to greet them as someone they can trust to help do a funeral. What was it Hazel said? Be personable, but not too personable. Don't be friendly, but don't be cold. Don't overstep; don't cross a boundary. Something like that.

The sound of conversation gets louder as I move through the house. I don't rush. I get a glass of water, and go and stand by the front door. God, the Moss looks different in the daylight. It looks grassy and inviting, like a meadow that's just a bit too flat, and has a suspicious, watery sheen to it. There's birdsong. Insects catching the yellow light. It shouldn't be beautiful here. Everything seems like watercolour paint slurred together until all the colours wash into one. But I find that I'm moved by it, in a very deep part of me.

I play with my phone while I'm standing there, so it doesn't look awkward. I bring up Ana's profile, and read the RIP messages. What else?

They must have driven up here in a convoy first thing this morning. I recognise Rebecca, from the café in Stirling, in the same denim jacket with the enamel pins on it, this time worn over a long dress that's in danger of soaking up mud from the damp grass. Her primary-teacher warmth and her casual tactility are on display here again, but this time they're being properly appreciated. Her friend, a woman who I haven't seen before, looks genuinely upset. She's wiping her eyes under her glasses while Rebecca strokes her arm and coos comforting words that I can't hear from where I'm standing, her phone in her other hand.

They stand grouped closely together; for a moment they all seem to be moving in unison, or not quite unison—like they're all connected somewhere, like a bunch of animals tied together at the tail. None of them are how they normally are; I don't need to know them to know that. All of them are off-kilter, not spinning on their proper axes; you can tell by the movements, the fumbling, the lack of balance. There's what, six of them, seven? I was expecting more. But it's not the relief that it should be. A smaller group surely requires me to give more of myself; more engagement, more intimacy. Keep your distance. Maintain the boundary. Be kind, but not too kind.

They'll resent that you're a woman.

And I see it happening. A couple of them notice me at once; looking up from a phone here, a cigarette there. And there's a look on their faces that reminds me of kids meeting strangers for the first time. It isn't distrust; it certainly isn't fear. But they're looking at me like something to be kept at a distance from. I see the boundary, then, almost as if it's a physical thing that I could reach out and touch. I'm here representing death, just like Hazel told me, and the boundary must be maintained. It makes me feel kind of powerful. That surprises me.

Rebecca looks up too, following the others' stares. For a minute, she just looks at me. Not surprised to see me exactly, but as if seeing me is a reality check of some kind. That's another thing that's important for me to remember; this is weird for everyone else too. Then she waves at me with the hand that's holding her phone, and I wave at her with the hand that's holding mine. I don't go up to them. I stand there by the door, as if I have a professional obligation to be standing there. Rebecca doesn't come over to me either, like her place is with the congregation, for now.

I don't know what I was expecting from a group of people who campaigned for a long-dead bog mummy to get a proper funeral. They look kind of normal, from this distance. But as I look at them, I start to see it; I start to see little strangenesses in them.

The group is mostly women, with only two men. Rebecca is maybe forty, but dresses a lot younger, with badges all over her denim jacket; I noticed she was trans when I first met her in Stirling, then felt bad for noticing. The woman Rebecca was comforting has tattoos all up her arm that are old and faded and look like ivy, or some other climbing plant. Her hair is blonde, and buzzed close to her scalp. Three different women have long grey hair. They stand apart from the others in their own group. A minute ago I thought I saw the two guys - both bald, both wearing glasses - holding or touching hands. There's some part of me that's a little embarrassed to be near them all, as if they might rub off on me somehow. I realise that I haven't eaten yet today. I haven't had coffee either. Maybe that's why I feel separate from what's around me. The disconnect clouds me, like ugly, opaque, unclean water, an old pond that's thickened with algae and fallen leaves.

There's wasps buzzing around us. They make me think of the bugs in my room that will be waiting for me when I go home. No matter what happens this weekend, no matter how the funeral goes, this break from reality will be over soon and I will still have bugs in my room when I go home. I watch them tumble and stutter, following them one at a time like picking a single raindrop to watch sliding down a window pane. And I see why there's so many of them. In a crack halfway up the wall, a quiet little mass of wasps is crawling and pulsing, like flies on rotten meat.

I flinch when one buzzes close to my ear. Rebecca sees me lurching away, and smiles at me, kind of sadly. The woman with tattoos who had been crying breaks looks over to where I'm standing, looking past me. She taps Rebecca on the shoulder and points. I look behind me back into the house to see what she's pointing at, and just in that moment, Hazel emerges from the gloom of the house.

The light hits her just right for a moment and there's something about the way her eyes and the bridge of her nose are illuminated by the daylight that makes me wish that I was seeing her for the first time, like these people are. She has a power to her.

I drop my gaze before she can look me in the eye; I don't know if I'm ashamed at having caught her praying, or if I'm embarrassed for her, or if I'm disappointed, kind of. If she acknowledges me or tries to greet me, I don't see it. She comes to stand by my side, her working hand holding onto her broken one. It would be so cold to the touch, that hand.

Rebecca pats her friend's arm one more time and comes towards us, looking like she knows she can't put it off any more. She smiles grimly at us both, greeting me as well as Hazel which I wasn't expecting; I didn't think she would consider us as two parts of the same thing.

Her eyes are a little wet. She runs her hands over her face as she comes over, then checks her palms for smudged makeup. "God," she says. "Thanks so much for being here. I know I said that already, but I really, really mean it. Both of you. Seriously." She laughs, and something catches in it. "I don't know why I'm getting emotional. Thank you. Sorry. Is now a good time to meet everyone, or do you have things to do first?"

Rebecca is looking at Hazel, but then she turns to me and touches me lightly on the shoulder, her long necklace jingling against the badges on her jacket, and whispers, "I'm so glad you're here," again, as if she doesn't want Hazel to hear.

"I actually need to borrow her for a moment. If that's okay." I see Hazel nod towards me off to my side. "One quick thing we need to take care of."

Something inside me sinks. My fingers fold closed and press into the heel of my hand, needing to feel something solid and hard inside me, pressing into the fleck of grit that's stuck there. It's close enough to painful to anchor me here.

"Of course," says Rebecca. "Absolutely. And I mentioned this briefly on the phone, but we clubbed together and got a couple of things for Mrs Ross, nothing big, nothing that would make her uncomfortable, just a bottle of wine and a plant and a sort of hamper thing, I just … it's so good of her to … " She waves her hands around, her bracelets clacking together. "I mean, you know. You know. I just don't want her to think we're not grateful. So, I'll grab you to talk about that later, maybe?"

Hazel nods and thanks her, and Rebecca hurries back to the group, all warm and ready to be embraced again. She's got sensible boots on under her skirt. She knows what she's here for.

When Hazel and I are left alone there's a second where I think she's about to bring up what I saw her doing. Then she looks at me, and looks at what I'm wearing. I didn't know what clothes to bring and I left it too late to ask anyone, so I've gone for all black; smart jeans, a long sleeve top with a polo neck. I look like event staff.

"You're still on for today, then?" She asks. "You still want to do it?"

I search her face for any hidden meaning. I don't know what she thinks would have changed between yesterday and today. She must be thinking that I only saw the bog mummy for the first time yesterday; she doesn't know that she's been following me for days now.

"Yeah. Definitely," I say, surprised by the conviction in my voice. Then, "If you still want me to."

She nods, curtly, squinting against the morning light. "I'll need to see you inside, then," she says.

"For what?"

"To interview you." And she indicates back towards the house with a flick of her head. I look where she's indicating, and then back at the congregation, and the wasps that flick around them, and won't leave them alone.

She looks at my face once, as if trying to read my expression, and then turns and heads back, not waiting for me to follow. Just before I turn to go after her, I catch a glimpse of the bog mummy, hanging on the edge of the group, watching me as if she thinks I'm talking about her behind her back. From here, it looks like the wasps are drawn to her, swarming around her as if she's their nest.

5

I watch Hazel move her shoulder as she walks down the hall, rolling it jaggedly backwards, trying to unstick a stuck muscle, ease out some tension. I wonder if she knows she's doing it. I can't help but feel the tension from her muscles spilling out and stiffening the air between us. The voices of the congregation follow us down the hall from outside. I'm walking a pace or two behind her, like I was last night, and it's strange to see her from this angle again in the daylight. She's skinny without her coat, and all angles. There's no holes in her ears for earrings.

She holds a door open for me, and cocks her head to indicate I go inside. "I'll be with you in a minute," she says. "I'm going to see if Morag's awake yet, she might want to sit in."

I realise that the room she's led me to is the room I slept in last night. And suddenly the thought of that is so intimate that it almost overwhelms me for a moment. But she closes the door behind her and is gone, leaving me alone in the room that I'd changed in, slept in, thought about Ana in.

I tidy everything away as quickly as I can. Everything that's mine gets bundled into my rucksack, which gets shoved into a corner. The blanket and pillows get pulled off the sofa and tidied away. It's back to being a study, or a small living room, or whatever it was before. Any clue that I spent the night here is gone. Then I sit down and look around, breathing slowly so Hazel won't see me nervous. The faded red sofa that I slept on sits uncomfortably against the green wall. I sink into it more than I feel like I should. I don't like to think that Hazel will be sitting in here with me, just me, sitting opposite me on the other sofa. I remember I still haven't eaten, and suddenly I'm worried about my breath. I try and swish saliva around my mouth like it's mouthwash.

The walls are dark green and covered in pictures, some of them in frames and some of them just stuck on the wall with drawing pins. There's some weird things tacked up there, pictures that look like maybe Morag did them herself; little collages made of scraps of magazines, paintings of abstract blocks of colour where the paint is applied too thickly, and coloured pencil drawings that remind me of girls I went to school with trying to draw anime characters, spending so long getting the eyes right that they'd fuck up the proportions.

There's too much crammed into this room; the arm of the faded red sofa sits pressed against a bay of shelves set into an alcove in the wall. There's a mess of books and folders stacked onto them, all at odd angles to one another. But on the lowest shelf, the one that's almost completely boxed in by the alcove and the arm of the sofa, there's a little set of speakers and— I lean over the arm of the sofa to get a better look—an old iPod Classic. Jesus. I haven't seen one of those for years.

I reach out to pick it up, and it's immensely heavy in my hand. It carries a horrible sadness to it, and for a second, I can't remember why. And then I turn it on, and see the silvery Apple logo on the screen, and I remember.

There was an after-school club that me and Ana used to go to when we were about eleven or twelve, that for some reason was in the crypt of a church in Hyndland. I went because Ana went; her parents made her go because they thought she didn't have enough friends, or something. But I went with her, which meant we only talked to each other. We would take control of the communal iPod Classic that played through bulky speakers, and sit scrolling through the songs, deciding what to play next. We didn't know about music. We picked the ones with the best titles, then fell about laughing if they were bad songs.

There was a sort of anteroom off the main space that was supposed to be a music room, but didn't have anything in it apart from a drum kit, so we would sit in there by ourselves and one or the other of us would try and play drums based on what we'd seen on tv. I was a bit better at it than her; she wanted to go crazy and do wild drum solos that lost their rhythm halfway and she just ended up crashing around making noise like a kid playing on pots and pans. I could keep rhythm. I could keep the bass drum going as I hit the snare and the hi hat in time, and the game when I was on the drum kit was to speed up slowly and see how long I could keep it going, like a tennis rally, before I slipped up and missed a beat somewhere. She would sit and grin at me as I got faster and faster, and giggle in delight when I almost messed up but caught it in time, and it was like something was being pulled tauter and tauter ready to snap, and my stress was her stress, and my excitement was her excitement.

Or we would hang about outside, in the little patch of paving stones between the car park and the fenced off churchyard, hanging on the fence, trying to climb it sometimes, racing each other, or just doing nothing, just half-ironically playing make believe and laughing at ourselves for being so stupid. We saw a cat once.

Are all happy memories of her going to be sad memories from now on? Is this how it's going to be, forever? Do I just go through life in the knowledge that a certain generation of iPod is forever going to make me sick with guilt?

It's plugged into the speakers, so I have to lean awkwardly over the arm of the sofa with my legs kind of pulled up underneath me to get to it. I hold it properly, in both hands, its familiar weight making something in me lurch. It's like a relic from deep history; its screen is tinted blue, its menu in that Apple font I remember so vividly. It seems so big now, so heavy. I scroll my thumb over the wheel and the iPod makes a clacking noise. And fuck, it's like getting a waft of a smell you remember from childhood. Suddenly you're there again. And then for no reason, just because I'm bored and because I like this old machine, I scroll the clicking wheel down to Shuffle Play.

It isn't loud when it comes on, which is a relief. Alone in the room, with the rain pattering against the window, I sit and listen for a moment. A man with a low and crunching voice singing about burning bridges down.

Footsteps pass the door and I stiffen, thinking it might be Hazel. They pass by, and I hear voices and more footsteps. It's the congregation. They've come indoors. As soon as I hear them I become aware of rain hitting the window behind my head, the window I slept next to last night, and suddenly it feels oddly claustrophobic; the thought of all those people forced inside by the rain.

When Hazel comes in again, she has her notebook in her hand, and she doesn't quite look at me all the way, as if she's embarrassed to be disturbing me. I'd be embarrassed too, walking in on me like this; I have my legs tucked underneath me and I'm half tipped over the edge of the sofa, still fingering the iPod as while I listen to this sad, slow song that sounds old and powerful.

It's like she's brought weather into the room somehow. I can't explain it. Not like thunderstorms, but like the tension in the air on a hot and overcast day. She's not a striking figure, especially not now with her coat gone, and what looks like a grey men's shirt swamping her, with its sleeves rolled up to her elbows. But I was right last night: she has a face for funerals.

I turn off the song as Hazel sits down in front of me, because to keep listening would be ludicrous. There's no greeting or anything like an introduction from Hazel; there never was. We haven't even shaken hands yet. She's left the door ajar, so that the sound of voices can be heard from elsewhere in the house. I look up, following the sound.

And my heart almost stops in my chest.

The face of the bog mummy is pressed up to the gap between the door and the frame. Pressed right up to it, so that her mouth, lips rotted all the way back to leave her teeth bare and menacing, touches the wood of the door. The sound of her breathing comes to me; slow and rattling, rasping at the dryness of her dead mouth. I don't think she has a tongue; I can hear the heavy sounds of her breath echoing in the cavern of a tongue-less mouth.

I catch Hazel's eye, looking at me, and I try to look relaxed, to breathe normally. My heart is beating so hard and so fast that I wonder if I might be dying. I swallow, as if that's going to do anything.

"How's Morag?" I ask, knowing my voice doesn't sound normal.

There's a little pause before Hazel answers. "She's fine. She takes a while to get up sometimes."

"How's she feeling about ... " I catch Hazel's eye. "You know. About today?"

Hazel doesn't say anything for a moment, getting something out of her pocket. I glance up at the door. The face is gone. I look back to Hazel. Then at the door again, just to check.

"She's had that dead body in her house about as long as I've been alive, did you know that?"

I don't say anything. I look at the door again.

"The thing about Morag ... " she shakes her head, "she's not well, Ali. I've seen her survive things most people wouldn't, but a life like hers takes a toll on a body." She pulls her hand out of her pocket and it's holding a little black notebook. She looks at it for a second. "You know that she's not made plans for the bog body, for when she goes. She won't entertain the idea of it. Sometimes she goes all misty-eyes and talks about finding someone to take over as its guardian, but I don't think she ever really means it. So this is good. This is the beginning of her loosening her hold on it. Getting used to the idea that it can't stay hers forever."

She hasn't looked me in the eye once since she started talking. She has an almost military gruffness to her now, that sits a little uneasily against the image of a narrow-shouldered woman with her wrists and ankles crossed, flicking open a neat little notebook with one hand.

She looks for a second like she's going to set her notebook down on the coffee-stained table between us, but then pauses, a little awkwardly, and sits it in her lap instead. The table is too low—I'd have been able to see in. She crosses one leg over the other to make a sort of table for the notebook, as she opens it to the right page. All of this done with one hand, of course. My eyes flick to the other one, lying motionless by her side. Then Hazel looks up at me from her notebook, gives me a thin-lipped grimace-smile, and gets right into it.

"So. There's a course that's run by the Humanist Society which is designed to prepare new celebrants for their careers. I'm wondering if you know about that already? It's not a requirement for the job, but for someone your age, with your lack of experience, it seems like the sensible first step for you."

I clear my throat. "Yeah," I say, trying to sit up as straight as possible. "I did actually think about doing that. It's just a lot of money right now; I looked into it and it wouldn't be covered by SAAS or anything. So it's kind of not an option for me."

Hazel nods, not looking up, as if this is the right thing for me to say. It makes me feel slightly proud of myself.

"It's also kind of … " I hesitate for a moment, not sure how to phrase it. "It's kind of not how I want to do it. It doesn't seem like the right way to start, for me."

She looks up at me, expecting me to clarify, but I don't say anything else. I shrug. That's all I've got.

"I'd be interested, in that case, to know what experience you have that you think would help you as a celebrant."

"Like what? Like other jobs? Um, I have like an actual CV that I could show you, if that makes things easier."

She looks at me very pointedly then. Her eyes are on me with that look she does that's like a bird of prey or a wild animal catching your eye and holding it for a second. Her eyes do have yellow in them. I wasn't imagining it.

"Ali, I've told you already what it is that this job requires of you. You're going to be in contact with one of the rawest edges of the human experience. To do this job effectively, you need an understanding of that which goes deeper than what can be taught. You need to be able to empathise. You need to be able to understand. That's the experience that I'm interested in."

The rain rattles against the window, like a roll on a snare drum. I hear the wind now, too.

"You're talking about death," I say quietly. Not a question. "You're talking about my experience with death."

Her eyes are on mine. Fixed. She doesn't say anything. Doesn't look away.

"Aren't you?"

She shrugs, as if it's the most natural thing in the world. "Would you be willing to share the experiences you've had with mourning?"

I look away and to the side. The rain drums. I feel my eyebrows furrowing like I'm trying to remember the answer to a difficult question. But I already know the answer.

"Take your time," she says.

I should tell her about the fish that I buried as a tiny child, by myself, without anyone telling me that I should do it, or telling me how. I should tell her about the bird that died in an instant, right in front of me and Ana, and the tribute we paid to it.

I scratch my forehead. "Um. Grandparents. Three grandparents, now. Well, one before I was born so that probably doesn't count. Then one when I was too young to go to the funeral or anything, or to really know what was happening if I'm honest. And it was my dad's dad, and I don't really see my dad, so it wasn't ... you know. Uh, and then my grandma when I was maybe fifteen. Or sixteen. That was like, that was a Catholic funeral and everything, and then the burial afterwards. And I, um ... "

I remember the smell of it. It's the only time in my life I've smelled the inside of a grave. It was a wet and thick smell, that seemed to come in layers. The smell of rain-logged ground, then of cut turf, then of the wet mud, and underneath it all the smell of cut-open, compacted earth that was six feet down. I should tell her this. But I don't. My hand flicks awkwardly to stop itself rubbing at the stone, like the movement of snapping fingers, without the finger snapping. I do it again.

"And there was a friend of mine. She died quite recently. That was sad."

"Did you go to her funeral?"

The world has moved very far away. Pondwater. I'm looking at it through pondwater.

"No."

"Why not?"

"I couldn't that day."

"Why couldn't you?"

"Work. I think. I don't really remember."

Everything is so far away. But I can feel something close to me. I can hear the breath of the bog mummy, like it's right in my ear.

"How did she die?"

"I don't want to—that doesn't matter, does it?"

"Okay. It doesn't matter. How did you mourn her, then? If you weren't at her funeral?"

I rub a hand over my face. I want to shove my fingers into the holes in my ears and rub the noise away like trying to rub away an itch at the back of your throat.

"Um. I just ... tried to think of the good memories we had. You know. Things like that. She was a good friend for a long time, so I just tried to … just tried to remember when we were really close. Remember her that way."

"Was there a time when you weren't close?"

I think I can smell it now. The grave-smell.

"Um. Yeah, I mean of course there was. We were friends when we were little and obviously people are going to change, they're going to change and grow apart cause that's what happens." The breathing is getting louder. I feel like I'm talking too loud, to be heard over it. "I mean … I mean I could show you a picture of her right now and you could see that we just weren't … we just weren't made of the same stuff by the end. You could just look at a picture of her and look at me, and you'd know just by looking at us."

The smell of the cut-open earth.

"Do you regret drifting apart from her?"

I rub at my face again. "She wasn't easy to be around. She did everything in the wrong direction, but like, on purpose."

"In the wrong direction?"

"I don't know what I mean by that … just like, the effort that most people put into being a certain way, she put the same effort into being the opposite. It got kind of, I don't know. Not annoying, but like … it's like my friend Sarah. She's great, I live with her. She's always wanting to like, better herself. And she really takes care of herself, you know, she always looks great and knows what to say around people. She used to be a lot heavier and didn't really know what she was doing with her life, and then she just kind of took charge of herself and turned it all around. And now she's really disciplined about things like food and uni and every-thing, like she can't … like she knows she can't slip up."

Animal eyes, again. There's a thought that's trying to manifest in my mind. I won't let it. I won't let it.

"You know, it's things like … she's really good at putting on makeup so that it doesn't look like she's wearing makeup, and doing her hair so it looks like it's just like that. And she knows to stand a certain way in company, and she knows to turn her body a certain way in pictures, to make herself look smaller. And like, her voice changes when she talks to boys, and she has a different smile for when she's talking to boys, that's almost like a kid's smile. And it's not even so they'll fancy her, it's also just like ... so that they won't hurt her. She has to do that, so that they won't hurt her. Do you know what I'm trying to say? It's so much work. She puts so much work into it. Every day. And living with her, being her friend, it's a reminder. It's a reminder that that's what I need to be as well, to, you know ... " I think for a moment, trying to find the right words. "To survive."

I don't even know what my hands are doing anymore. I clasp them between my knees to stop them moving, pressed together like they're in prayer.

"Ana—the one who died—she put all that effort in, and she made herself different. She built herself differently. Cause the thing is, you don't really win, do you? Even if you do all that stuff right, even if you do the work every single day, you're not ... you're still not good enough. And you're still not powerful, and the people who would hurt you or humiliate you for being ugly or strange, they're the same people who would hurt you and humiliate you for being too beautiful or too successful. You can do everything right and they'll hate you anyway. Maybe she thought she could win by not playing. So maybe if she made herself different, she would survive that way."

There's a moment where neither of us speak. And that silence between us is all it takes for the most awful thought I've ever held in my mind to rise up like dark water. Ana is in a grave. She is a dead body, and she has been buried in the earth. This is not temporary. Ana is in a box in the earth and she will never come back out of it, because she is dead, and she's going to be dead forever. She is going to be dead forever.

I feel like everything physical is swimming away from me. I've cut ties with my body and I can feel it get weaker, like there's nothing to hold it up. I do everything I can to bring myself back, but all I can do is hold myself steady, to swallow it down, like I've swallowed it down a hundred times before.

"Do you blame yourself for her death?" Hazel says.

It's like there's an intake of breath in the room around us. I almost think the rain stops hitting the window for a second or two. And then everything feels clear again; I'm a part of the room again, I'm in my body again. It feels sharp. Like a fingernail scraping on skin.

I give that animal look of hers right back to her.

There's a flash of something across her face. She holds her hand up. "Ali, what I mean by that is—"

I stand up. My legs are too close to the glass coffee table, so it scrapes on the wooden floor. The glass top is loose from the frame, and it rattles alarmingly, which makes Hazel lurch out and grab it, knocking her notebook off her lap. There's a moment when we just stand there, me looking down at her and her looking up at me.

I walk past her without saying anything and open the door to leave. I'm going now. I'm going home. I'll get a bus from the village or something, doesn't matter. Fuck it. I need to leave.

"Ali, wait—"

It's nothing to her. Loss is nothing to her. I feel myself running my hands over my face as I go, trying to keep everything in place, pushing everything back down, that vibration under the skin that's threatening to burst out. I don't storm out. I don't slam the door behind me. I don't say what I want to say.

The only thing that matters is that I get out of this house; I don't look where I'm going, don't consider that anyone might be following me, or anyone might be blocking the way, until I look up and I almost scream at what's looking back at me.

She's there. The bog mummy. In front of me, standing between me and the way out. She's breathing loudly; I can see it happening in the muscles between her ribs, the dead flesh that used to be her lungs ballooning and contracting as she stares straight at me from the dead centre of the hallway. For a moment I just stand facing her, and she stands facing me. Her papery, empty eyelids start to twitch and flicker like she's trying to get them open.

I'm not even sure what it is I do, then. I just go, I just rush past her and don't look back, can't look back, just have to get out, to keep going, keep going until I get to where she can't follow me, until I'm through the open front door, out of the house, out into the wilderness and the rain.

6

The bog, in the rain and the cloud-covered dullness of the rainstorm, is vaster than any place on earth has the right to be. It's a skyless hole in the world. It goes on forever and ever in each direction, fading into grey on all sides, and I am alone. My limbs are heavy, like they're giving up already. Better just to sink. Get it over with. I've stopped watching my step in the bog. I've stopped caring. I feel like I've walked for hours and haven't moved.

I feel lost in a way that I've never felt lost before; lost like an astronaut whose tethers have been cut. I wish it was true, now; I wish there were creatures lurking in the marshlands with lanterns. I wish they'd come and take me into the earth to drown.

I close my eyes and I try to remember Ana, try to shake the image of her in a coffin in the ground, try to remember her as a person. But she doesn't come. The comfort I want from her isn't coming. I want to remember when she made me laugh, or when she liked a film that I made her watch, or when she went on a long and manic tangent about a song or a TV show she was obsessed with, but there's nothing coming to me. So I force past that; I force past the memories that make me happy and find what's buried deeper.

It was the night we went to the concert in the Grand Ole Opry. I think that was my last chance to hold on to our friendship, that night. That was the night when I decided to let it go. But this was before all that; before the walk home, before she told me about the skin on her nipples and I knew I couldn't keep this up.

I was in a good place, for a minute. For a minute, during the break between the opener and the singer we'd come to see, I was feeling things properly, and letting myself be moved by the place we were in, and the way it wore its quaintness and campness so openly and with such pride.

She could have said anything to me, in that minute. Anything in the world.

"You know that every time I'm back in Glasgow I get this horrible paranoia that everyone we went to school with can see my Tinder profile. Like one of those awful wee boys who used to ask me if I had a pussy or a cock will just be swiping around and then they'll see me, and they'll screenshot it and send it to their friends." She shuffles up in her chair and puffs out her chest, putting on a voice like the young men who'd shouted at her from across the street earlier today, "Like, 'look at the fucking state of it, look at its fucking hair, oh my *god*. What's it wearing? Where's its tits gone?'" She took a drink, grinning at me a little awkwardly over the rim of her glass. "Not to say that I wouldn't fuck any of them if we matched. Remember Calum McCready from our year, the one who broke that gay kid's leg? Have you seen him lately? He is a beautiful, aggressive little man these days. He's like a well-bred show dog. Face like a Pekingese on that boy. Honestly? I would."

She drank deeply again. "I could set it to just girls, I suppose. I mean, the really fucking awful girls we went to school aren't going to find me on Tinder, are they? Unless they're all gay now, and it was all a projection of their internalised homophobia all along. Which, fair fucks if that's the case. But maybe that's the way to do it. Cut the dick out of my life for a wee while, curb the paranoia."

She took one long drink, finishing her pint, then looked at the empty glass as if there might be something in there that she'd missed. "I never really ask you about dating and sex and stuff, do I? Is that just me being selfish, or do you like, not ever want to talk about it?"

I had already started not telling her things. Even the big things that I wanted so desperately to tell her about, that I had to remind myself to keep from her. I wanted to tell her how it had felt when I tried it for the first time with a boy Sarah had introduced me to, how outside myself I had to go just to get through it without telling him to stop. I wanted to tell her that I know the implications of that; that I thought I knew something about myself now that was likely to impact the rest of my life about as much as having part of a limb amputated. And I wanted to ask her, what if I tried it with a girl and I didn't like that either, what the fuck would that make me?

"I don't ask you about yourself a lot these days, do I?" she asked.

I shook my head, not looking at her, letting a drop of condensation on my glass drop coldly onto my finger. "It's me who's done that. Not you."

"How come?"

I shrugged. "I don't really like opening up to people these days, you know? It just makes things easier if I don't."

She didn't say anything. She was still swirling the nothing around at the bottom of her pint glass, watching it and waiting for me to continue.

"I keep tabs on everything I do. I have to watch to see what my hands are doing, all the time, in case I have mannerisms I don't notice that other people notice. It's like I have to be aware of the muscles in my face all the time in case I make expressions that I don't mean to make. It's like if I don't watch myself, all the time, something is going to slip through. And someone's going to see something. Someone's going to see me for exactly what I am."

"And what's that?"

"I don't know."

And I looked at her looking into my face with her eyes big and brown and set deep in those dark circles that were there all the time now. I looked at her just being everything I was so scared to be. Being everything that I was disgusted with in myself. Being it so wonderfully. She dug the grit out of her body. I couldn't. I didn't say anything to her because I didn't know whether to tell her I was proud of her or that I was so scared for her it made me kind of hate her. There was no point in saying either. They were both true.

And somehow I knew then that she felt all of that too, all of that turned around and pointed at herself.

And I could feel that pride and that fear and that hatred beaming out of her. She couldn't keep it in. There had always been too much of her to be kept in. She'd never been skinny, or small; always too much in one body, but wearing it well. Like a strong animal. Her face had a roundness to it that might have been soft, but its features were strong and prominent; her lips, nose, eyebrows, all big and eye-catching. And I remember looking at her then, at her dark eyes and her strangeness and her hair that was tousled and short, and knowing right then that whatever she was, I was the same. Like a baby looking in a mirror and realising for the first time that it's staring at itself. I'd never felt anything more powerful or more frightening before.

"But what's left after that?" Ana said.

I swallowed, my mouth suddenly dry and almost numb. "I don't think there's anything left. But that's okay. I'd rather not be anything."

She looked at me for a long time. She said, "Stick that on a dating profile. See what you catch with it."

I know for certain now that the bog mummy has followed me out of the house, in some primal, animal part of me. She's coming after me. My heart thumps in my neck. It's like the sky has vanished in the thick, smothering cloud, like it's turned its head so as not to see. She is out here with me.

I move faster, further away from the house and into the grey, lurking flatness of the Moss. The clouds have come down to settle on the ground now, casting everything in a stinging cold mist that seems to have a solidity that it shouldn't have, like if you were to touch it, it would have the weight and physicality of silk or muslin. It's cold. My breath puffs in front of me in shorter and shorter clouds as the panic rises.

The last time I saw her, the very last time, I saw her at a party that I'd gone to with Sarah and Sarah's friends. I didn't know she was going to be there, and something heavy and cold had dropped in my stomach when I saw her across the busy, smoky living room. I went over to her, of course; I gave her a half-hearted hug, and I half-heartedly introduced her to Sarah and the rest of the girls I had come with, the girls who I would leave with to go to Garage and drink Malibu and coke until I was drunk enough to kiss boys and not mind it. We hadn't spoken in months. Not since the concert. Not since she told me about the skin on her breasts, and the angry colour of the flesh underneath, and I'd seen myself reflected in her like a fairground mirror. I wished she hadn't been there.

I asked how she was, and she asked how I was, and then I made my excuses and went with Sarah's friends to talk to some guys they knew. If I'd spent any real time talking to her, I would have had to explain to the nice girls in New Look dresses from Sarah's business studies course how I knew someone like that. If I'd acted like we were real friends, they'd start to think things about me that I didn't want them to think.

As I was getting ready to leave with my new friends, I caught Ana's eye across the busy hall of the big west end flat. She was waiting in the line for the toilet, still holding her drink, leaning against the wall with her patterned shirt buttoned up to her throat and her chest flattened out awkwardly by the sports bra she always wore. I caught her eye and she held up her drink to me, tipping her plastic cup to me in a gesture that was so singular, so utterly full of character that I suddenly remembered her getting up from the red gravel after having been pushed down, and swooping a bow like it was all a joke that she had been in on all along. And then I couldn't help but remember the red of her cut open knees, and that made me think of the pink insides of her nipples where the skin split apart. And I felt a surge of revulsion towards her that I'd never felt for anyone before. And I wondered then if I could fix her, like I'd fixed myself. And if she would hate me for trying.

And then I turned and left in the bubble of laughing, chatting girls that for my own protection I had decided to be the same as. And that was the last time.

I'm not looking where I'm going; I feel like paying attention to things like distance and direction would be a waste of time, because distance and direction so clearly don't have meaning any more; not out here. The bog doesn't think in terms of tangible physical space, I know that know; and I'm sure it doesn't care about time, either. That's how the mummy ended up slipping so seamlessly into our century from her own with flesh still on her bones. Maybe this was how it happened. Maybe she walked to far into the bog, slipped between time and the wet ground, and was transformed by it. Maybe that's what's going to happen to me.

I feel my pace quickening even as the ground gets more and more difficult to navigate and it seems like every second step is a slip off of solid ground and into water, or squelching mud, and I don't even care any more, because I know that I can't let her catch up with me. I know that I have to do anything in my power to get away from her.

And that's when I stop in my tracks.

Stretching out in front of me, in long, uneven rows, are hundreds of pits dug into the ground. Rectangles of pure darkness. Pure black. Rows and rows of them, stretching into the bog, demolishing the land. Morag, her wet hair and the spade. They're graves. They're empty graves cut into the bog. It comes to me again, the smell of my grandmother's grave. The smell of Ana's grave.

That's when my legs stop working. I can't go any further. I stop, and breathe, hard and painful into the raw and suffocating fog. And I know beyond a shadow of a doubt, panting into the grey air, that this is where she finds me. This is where I turn around and she's slouching towards me on legs that are too spindly and weak to hold her up properly; she'll be half sunk into the bog, pulling each foot out from where it's been sucked into the mud with every step, her hands held out in front of her, reaching.

"Ali?"

I don't turn around.

"It's really wet out here, Ali. Do you want to come inside?"

I don't believe it's her. I don't believe it's Hazel. What if this is how she gets me? She tricks me into thinking she's someone I can trust, then as I turn round to look at her ...

I turn round anyway. It is wet. The stray bits of hair that have fallen out of Hazel's messy ponytail are stuck to her face by the rain, cutting dark, wavering lines across her brow and cheeks. They look like they've been drawn on. Like ancient war paint.

"What are those?" I point in front of me.

"It's the peat. Where Morag cuts it out of the bog. Those are the trenches there, and that's the peat that's been dug out. You see over there?"

I look where she's pointing, and there's a low stack of what I suppose must be slices of earth, sitting like a cairn of stones off to one side.

"They look like graves," I say.

She shrugs. "I suppose."

I turn to face the pits again. I can't make sense of them. I can't make sense of how they look, cut into the waterlogged ground. Some of their edges are crumbling, some of the earth too soft to hold its shape. They must be deep, to hold their shape. They must be cut so deep into the earth.

"Was she the one who found it?" I ask, not quite wanting to turn my back to the holes in the earth. "Was Morag the one who found the bog body?"

Hazel looks at her feet and repositions herself on the wet ground. "She found it in the trench she dug at the back of the house. The one I showed you."

I think of the body hiding in the ground, its teeth bared and grinning.

"Ali, I want to say sorry, for what I said in there," Hazel says. "I pushed too hard. I apologise. I get that bit wrong sometimes. I get the people part wrong."

She's picked a long piece of grass and is worrying it between her finger and thumb. Then, seeing me looking, she wipes the wet hair from her forehead with the back of her hand. "It matters to me how people feel about someone they've lost. It matters to me how they grieve, and how they remember them. And I thought, if you'd had a chance to talk that through, and put it into words, then it might help you. If you found the words to talk about your own loss, it would help you find the words to help other people through their losses. I'm sorry, Ali." She looks up from the blade of grass, at me. "I really am."

"I found out from a Facebook post," I tell her. "I just opened Facebook to see what my friends were saying about, I think it was *Line of Duty*, or something like that. I looked, and there was this post that came up on my wall 'cause she was tagged in it. And it said like, I can't believe you're gone. RIP. Something like that. And I clicked on it, and it took me to her page, and … there were all these RIP messages. Tagging her in them like she was going to see them. And that was how I found out."

I run my sleeve over my eyes even though I'm not crying. "You think I could stretch that out for a whole sermon?"

"I think it's a start."

There's a silence. The rain has started to ease up. "Why were you running?" she asks.

"I just scared myself," I tell her. But she's looking at me with an openness I haven't seen in her before. Her head is tilted slightly and there's something in the way her eyebrows are furrowed and her eyes are wide that's so earnest it's almost funny. So I laugh, feeling my mouth taking on the shape of the bog mummy's mouth, and not knowing how to stop it. I think about her smiling out of the earth, and how charged with energy the ground is here.

"It's ... I mean it's the fucking bog mummy. What else is it going to be? She follows me around. I don't know how to make her stop. I don't know if she's ever going to leave me alone now, and I'm scared. She makes me kind of ... scared."

I look up at Hazel and she's looking right at me. Not in confusion, not in sympathy. Her eyes are wide and flickering. The wind's picked up. It flicks and paws at us as we stand opposite each other. And look at her, she doesn't know what to say to that; she's balled up that bit of grass and tossed it to the side trying to wipe the green off her hand on the sleeve of her coat. But it's too late. Something's changed. I've let something spill open between the two of us, and things aren't going to be the same now.

"You too, then?"

She nods, as her hand comes to her temple to keep the dark hair off her face. "You're frightened of her?" she asks.

I nod. I almost think I feel tears pricking my eyes.

"I was, too. At first."

"Then what happened?"

Hazel laughs and looks down, like she's embarrassed. "I realised … I realised I was objectifying her. I was reducing her to a body. I was reducing her to that awful, abject shape that survived the bog. She isn't just a body, any more than you or I are just a body. The difference is, ours are occupied, for now. And when we're gone, we'll have people to vouch for the fact that we were alive once, and we were nuanced, complicated people, not just flesh and gristle. That we were souls, that occupied a body for a little while," she smiles thinly again. "Although Morag did warn me not to get religious today. She's got a thing about that."

I turn towards the rows of empty graves again, that aren't graves at all.

"That's why I have to know about your friend. I have to know who she was, and I have to know what she meant to you. One day all that's left of us is the way people remember us."

"Her name was Ana." The cold of the air has started to numb my face. I can't feel my lips.

"Ana," she says, giving the name the reverence it deserves. And then, softy. "Do you want to stay out here for a minute?"

I nod. The rain's eased off, but the sky is thick and heavy, like it's taking a deep breath before starting up again. The cold has started to prickle, but I like being out here, with Hazel. I think I like how the fog and grey sky makes the bogland look; like it's ancient and a little mystical, like we've slipped through a crack some-where and into a world that isn't ours.

And then of course, there she is again. The bog mummy did follow me, as it turns out; she's ambling towards us now, looking up at me like she knows she's upset me. She walks just as awkwardly and unnaturally as I predicted, but with a sheepishness and care when navigating the bog that betrays how aware she is of her own limitations. She's a corpse, after all. But Hazel's right; she should be more than that. My heart suddenly gets all heavy, looking at her picking her way through the difficult ground. No one remembers her as anything other than this.

We begin to move back towards the house now, Hazel and I. The bog body is following behind us, and I check over my shoulder to make sure we're not leaving her behind.

"I think ... " Hazel says, with an uncertainty I haven't heard before. "I think this will do something for her. For the bog mummy. The funeral, the ceremony, it ... I don't think it's just for show. I think there's some part of her that hasn't quite died. That's been kept here, tied to the land somehow. I know that isn't what

Morag believes, and I'm sure it isn't what you believe either. That's okay. But I want you to know, Ali, that I've seen things happen in my life and in my line of work that have made me quite sure that there are forces at work in this world beyond our understanding. I am quite sure. I don't understand these forces any better than you or anyone else, and I don't pretend to. But I believe … I believe that we'll be helping her today. I think we'll be putting her to rest."

We walk quietly for a few more paces. We're almost at the house, now. I thought I'd gotten myself so unbelievably lost.

Then Hazel says quietly. "I really thought it would be both hands, you know."

7

Before she goes to wake Morag, Hazel makes me sit in the living room in the warmth while she goes into the kitchen, where the congregation is chatting quietly. I hear her voice join theirs for a few minutes. Then she brings me out a cup of tea and some toast and peanut butter, without saying anything and without really looking at me. Then she touches the radiator to make sure it's warm, and turns it up.

She lingers for a minute, before going off to Morag's room. "I keep going back to what you said about your flatmate, back there. In the interview."

"Oh. God. I didn't really know what I was saying."

She leans against the radiator. "I'm trying to re-member something I read once about a snake," she says. "There's a Greek myth about a murderer who ran an inn, or something. He made people lie on an iron bed and if they were too small to fit the bed, he'd stretch them on a rack or beat them out like metal until they fit. If they were too tall, he'd cut off their feet. Because the whole point of the bed was that there was no way to win. Nobody fit the bed." She cocks her head, trying to think. "I feel like there was something about a snake in there, too. I think the only one who ever fit the bed was a snake."

"Why a snake?"

She draws the looping shape of a snake with her hand, staring at nothing. "They're like liquid. They take the shape of whatever space they're in. They contort without doing damage to themselves."

There's another quiet space.

"They used to think snakes were immortal, didn't they?" I ask.

She nods, a little grimly. I hear the congregation putting plates and cutlery out in the kitchen. Without saying goodbye, she slips out of the living room door to go and see to Morag.

When she's gone, I stand up and run my hand through my drying hair to get the worst of the tangles out. I don't feel the need to check my appearance in the bathroom mirror. I already know what I look like when I've been out in the rain.

I go through to the kitchen where Rebecca sits with the congregation. The kitchen table is long, and covered in a worn and faded floral tablecloth. It's pressed up against a wall, and the seven members of the congregation sit bunched together on the one side. They must have brought food with them when they came, they must have borrowed chairs from other rooms. I wonder how many of them believe what Hazel believes? I imagine most of them do; if not in a strictly religious or spiritual way, I'm sure everyone sat around this table is here to see the bog mummy put to rest, just like Hazel is.

I say hi, and they look up one by one, greet me warmly, introduce themselves. I spend a little time talking with them. I get to know their names, and how they know each other. They tell me what jobs they do and who arranged to bring the food for today. They talk over each other, bounce off one another. They make each other laugh. But I stay at the door, with my hands around my tea. I know there has to be a boundary between me and them. But the bog mummy is here by my side, and only I know it.

After a little while I make my excuses and go back to the room where I slept last night. It's well into the afternoon now, but I have a feeling that the funeral won't be starting while the sun is in the sky.

I turn on the iPod again and lie down on the sofa; I'm exhausted, I realise, more tired than I've maybe ever felt. I've buried my phone in my bag. It feels strange to just be lying down and waiting for time to pass without my phone or my laptop. But the bog mummy sits on the sofa opposite me, and I watch her sway along to Morag's music. I smile at her. Then I go to sleep.

A little while later, a knock at the door wakes me up. I hear Hazel's voice.

"Ali," she says, quietly. "She wants to see you."

Morag is curled up in bed, looking incredibly old. I smell the mustiness of her dressing gown. She looks like an ox or buffalo, something shaggy and unclean, big and almost formless, but with the striking vulnerability that those huge strong animals have, with their big, kind eyes, and the knowledge that they're still prey for sharper, faster things.

"There she is," she growls warmly at me, with a grin that cracks her wonderful face.

"How are you feeling?" I ask, hovering near the door. I shouldn't be seeing her like this. She makes a throaty noise in response.

And then I realise that Hazel hasn't quite come into the room with me. She's standing at the door with her hand on the doorknob. She looks at me and smiles, the lines at the sides of her mouth creasing. Then I see Morag give her something like a nod, and she slips out of the room, gently pulling the door closed behind her.

The bog mummy, in the room with me, meets my eye anxiously.

I hold my cup of tea close to me for a second, not quite knowing what to do or say. She shuffles herself up into more of a sitting position, shoving at the pile of pillows behind her as she does so. Her breathing is so loud, and so laboured.

There's a drop of tea hovering on the rim of my mug. I rub it away with my thumb. "Are you feeling okay about today?"

This time there's a long pause before she answers.

"It feels like this is me saying goodbye to her." She shakes her head; slowly, like it's desperately heavy. "I tried to protect her. That's all I wanted. I didn't care about making money from her, I didn't care about putting her on show. I just wanted her here. I wanted her to be somewhere they couldn't ... " She waves her hand and furrows her brow like she's in pain. "Where they couldn't bless her and put her back in the ground. I didn't want them to say prayers over her, I didn't want them getting near her with their incense and their holy water, locking her up in a box and covering her up with hallowed dirt. As if she hadn't spent enough time in there already. 'Cause I think about her, Ali, when she was alive; our iron age girl, living out here at the dawn of Christianity, or in the dying throws of whatever paganism came before it. And either way it's a life that's just utterly beholden to terrible, terrible religion."

She glances up at me. "There's things you'll find out about her, Ali. About that poor girl, and what they did to her. Those holy men." She scoffs, darkly. "Imagine it, Ali. Imagine being stuffed into the earth for a thousand years because of what holy men did to you, and you're dug back up to find out that there's still unspeakable things being done to girls in the name of one god or another."

She's gone glassy eyed. The curtains on her window are open; the grey sky and the ragged landscape meet her eye as she stares for a minute, expression gone slack, not blinking.

Then she shakes her head and the moment's broken.

"And Hazel," she says. "That girl. What are we going to do with her? All the terrible pious scum that I've had the misfortune to rub up against in my life, and she's more convinced of a world beyond our own than any of them. She's obsessed, Ali. Her and her bloody hand. I almost watched her destroy her life for it, and that's not an exaggeration, pet. She once tried to copy the behaviour patterns of everyone who's had a religious experience. Went through them all one by one, anyone who was visited by an angel, anyone who saw the Blessed Virgin on a tea towel. She burned herself on an open fire once. To get a little Joan of Arc.

"And I was there for her through it all, even when she didn't want me there. I was there waiting, ready to take care of her, ready for when she'd come and cry into my arms again with the great, suffocating terror of it all. I was there.

"And she won't … god, Ali, she just won't see it for what it is. She doesn't see what the harm it does to people, won't see it for the violent, misogynistic, repressive force it is. She's got the proof she needs. No one's going to change her mind, now."

She holds out her hand to me. I go over and take it, putting my mug down on the bedside table that's cluttered with balled up tissues and scattered bits of jewellery and empty blister packs. She doesn't squeeze it, doesn't hold it too hard. When she speaks again, she speaks very quietly.

"You look a bit bedraggled, love. Have you been out?"

"I saw the place where you dug the peat out of the ground. I … it kind of freaked me out to be honest. It looked like graves."

She turns to look at me over her fleecy shoulder. Her eyes are small, smaller than they usually are, the way plants shrivel and shrink in the winter. "It's a wee bit obsessive, isn't it? A wee bit like I'm trying to punish the ground for something." She laughs. "I'm not. I promise I'm not. It's just … " She sighs heavily. Runs her thumb over the back of my hand. "Sometimes it's like I need to put my hands to something or else I don't know what I'll do. It's something my body's good for, do you understand? My generation, growing up, we didn't get told that womens' bodies could be good for something. Except having babies, of course. It feels good, looking out into that bog, and knowing that I did that, with this body. It makes it feel like it's mine."

The rain has started again; I can hear it against the window. I feel a very, very sad tranquillity, that isn't far away from joy. I don't speak, because I have nothing to say, and I know there's nothing she needs to hear.

"This body's been through a lot, you know. It felt for a long time like it belonged to just about anyone apart from me."

The bog mummy shuffles closer to Morag, and I almost think she's about to reach out and touch her. Morag crinkles up in a sad little smile, as if she can sense her, too. I love her, I think. I could imagine knowing her all my life, this boulder of a woman, her hands calloused and strong from years and years of digging holes. She draws her slipper-socked feet into herself, away from the side of the bed, clearing space, inviting me to sit.

I sit down on the bed and she tucks her feet against me, curling her toes up against my leg. She turns my hand over in hers and rubs my palm with her thumb.

"What's that?"

"Oh. That's always been there, it's like … " I clear my throat. I've never actually had to explain what it is to anyone before. "It's a bit of gravel that just got stuck in there one day. It's been there since I was like, eight or nine."

She leans over, elbow on the bedside table, and takes my hand in both of hers, pressing down gently with her thumb to feel the stone, careful not to press too hard. She doesn't say anything, doesn't look up. She peers closer, intently. Her breath moves the strands of her hair that have fallen in front of her face. Then she lets go and sits back, still looking at my hand.

I fold my hand over to rub it, instinctively.

"Hazel tell you about her hand?" she asks.

"The one that she can't use?"

Morag nods slowly, something different in her expression that I can't quite place.

"What was it, like an illness or something?"

"I don't really know what it was, exactly. Not in medical terms. Something to do with nerve damage I think, but … " There's a strange pause. "It's a bit of an odd story. The way she tells it, anyway." She nods at my hand. "How did the grit get there? You fall?"

"Yeah."

She winces sympathetically. "Must have quite the fall to lodge something in that deep."

"Yeah. But the gravel comes from this pitch that doesn't exist any more, so it's like, well at least there's this bit left. This bit got stuck in me and survived."

She smiles. Her small teeth are slightly yellowed, like old ivory. "I like that. Was it worth preserving, that place?"

I think of Ana. I think of the two us huddled small together in the vast red landscape; our place, for years and years. "Yeah."

148

She thinks. Gives me a look, then looks away and nods slowly, with a thin, wry smile. "Preserved in your body. Like our friend was preserved in the ground." She slips her hand out of mine, and gently lifts some speck of dirt or dead insect out of my damp hair.

"Shall I tell you, then? Shall I tell you the story of Hazel Weir's right hand?"

"I don't know much about who she was before she came here, and I don't imagine I ever will. But I know a little. I know it was somewhere in Ireland that was remote, somewhere that was isolated, and somewhere that was stuck in its ways. Lot of god, in a place like that. The insidious, all-encompassing kind of god, that sticks in you like a splinter; one that you can never pick out of you once the skin grows over. It sticks in you and spreads, and if you don't catch it, it finds its way to your brain and tricks you into thinking it was your idea all along. And that does something to a child, that splinter of a god. It polices your thoughts and your impulses, and lays claim to your body.

"She was seventeen when she got herself over here, when I found her. A skinny wee girl with these wild staring eyes and all this mad, dark hair, frail and powerful like an injured bird of prey.

"She was pregnant, Ali. That was the thing. And I don't know who ... I don't know how it happened. Probably some half-feral boy from a farm somewhere that she saw something of herself in, without a thought to the consequences. I hope that's who it was. But whatever the circumstances, she had something growing in her, Something she didn't want there.

"So. She must have heard somewhere that you have to run away across the Irish sea to get that problem sorted, cause she knows she can't have this thing inside of her, can't let it grow, can't have it leech off of her and come into being. But—and this is the bit that I'm a little unclear on, just so's you know—there's some combination of her using up all her money to get over here in the first place, and a contact she thought she had in Scotland apparently not existing after all—but she finds herself stranded here. And the thing is, she hasn't been eating, hasn't been sleeping, she's been drinking like a sailor to try and wash this thing out of her, and she's half-delusional with it all. If it's not a breakdown then it's something fucking close.

"So she just ... wanders. Walks the earth. Homeless. Sleeping rough if she sleeps at all, stowing away on buses and trains with no idea where she means to go. She won't tell me for how long; might have been weeks. Christ, it might have been months.

"And all the while, she's praying. Not to that bitter old Catholic god she grew up with, no, he never did any good for her: it's something older she's praying to, something more feral, something that doesn't have a name, doesn't have form in her mind. And as she wanders, as she starts to meander further and further north, further and further away from cities and people and the rational world, she starts to feel it all the stronger. But all the while she's getting sicker and weaker and bloating with this thing in her belly that isn't going anywhere. So her prayers turn to bargaining. She's saying, to this god, this force, whatever it is; she's saying she'll give it anything if it takes this baby away. And she's got nothing left to bargain with but her body so it's all, I'll give you one of my ribs, I'll give you a kidney, I'll give you my eyes.

"Now, this all went on, what, fifteen years ago? Give or take? I was still strong enough to leave the house in those days. To go out into the world. And she had gotten herself to some farm somewhere, I can't remember where, where I'd been working as a labourer. And this the way she tells it, the way she's always told me: as she's wandering the land, barely able to even stand by this point, there's one last prayer she sends out with her last little scrap of strength before she collapses of exhaustion. *Take away this baby and I'll give you my hands.*

"And then, I don't know what happened to her, whether she collapsed, or had a fall, or ... I thought she was dead when I found her. I came with her in the ambulance when they took her to the hospital. I never really left her after that. She was alright of course, in the end; it took them some time but they fixed her up as good as they could be expected to. The thing is, Ali, from the cold or the malnutrition or the exhaustion or whatever it was, well the shock and the damage it did; she miscarried. And the only other real injury was damage to the nerves in her right hand. As if all the nerves were cut, like it was still there but severed at the root. It's dead weight now, that hand. Like something reached down and plucked it out of itself.

"The way she sees it, something took her up on the bargain she made that day out in the wilderness. Someone got rid of the baby, and took her right hand as payment. And that was the proof, for her. That right there was the proof she needed."

Morag's voice is low. "Faith is a strange thing. I think believing that there's something bigger than us out there in the universe isn't always a comfort. Especially when you owe it a hand."

I don't say anything. I follow Morag's gaze to the darkening sky outside the window.

"I don't think I can do it."

"What, pet? What can't you do?"

"The, uh … the funerals. Being a celebrant. I don't know why I thought I'd be good at it. The idea of talking to people about their dead loved ones. Being kind about it, but having that remove you need to have. Not getting upset about it. Like, I just tried to talk to Hazel about a friend of mine that died and I … like, I genuinely got so upset that I had to storm out of the room and go stand in the rain for a bit. So yeah. That was my plan, and it's … I can't do it. So I don't know what I'm going to do now. I have genuinely no idea what I'm going to do with my life."

Morag sits forward, and rearranges her pillows in silence for what seems like a long time. Then, when she's comfortable, she turns to me again. "What's keeping you in Glasgow, pet? Is it your mum and dad, your family? You got a job there, got friends there? What's in Glasgow to stop you leaving?"

She knows the answer. "There's nothing really keeping me anywhere to be honest."

"No anchor there? Nothing you couldn't let go of if something came up?"

I shake my head.

"And if I were to offer you a responsibility that would take you away from there for good. What would you think of that?"

This takes a second to land. I look at her, to see if she's being serious.

She shuffles round to face me full on, serious now. "Ali, pet, I wouldn't ask if I didn't think you could do it, if I didn't think it'd suit you and it'd bring you happiness of a kind. And you can say no, of course you can say no, you can turn me down and I won't be angry at you, I'll understand, I promise. But we both know there's nothing for the likes of us out there in the world when the ones that loved us are gone. That's the sad truth of it, petal, and we're the ones that only a handful know how to love."

She reaches out and takes a strand of my hair, and runs it through her fingers to the end. "Come live here when I'm dead, Ali. Come and stay away from everyone and guard my old girl from the world. You don't have a place in the world anymore, so stop trying. Be what I am, pet. Be nobody, live a nothing life in the middle of nowhere. Shrug it all off and be nothing."

I don't know how to meet her eye. My flat, my room, Sarah, my phone, the dust on my laptop screen and the insects that crawl out of my carpet flicker like afterimages of a dream. I could disappear from all of it and not say a word to anyone. Leave them to wonder where I'd gone.

"People are so cruel, Ali. Even when they don't mean to be. I want you to be happy. I want you to be somewhere safe from them, somewhere out of their reach, where their rules don't matter. You can say no. You can say no, petal, if that's what you want. But the offer's there. We'll just leave it there on the table for now, will we?"

She squeezes my hand one more time, and then I hear the door opening behind me. I turn to look at Hazel, and I know that she's come to take us to the funeral. My mouth feels suddenly dry, looking at her now; her one working hand on the doorknob, the one she sold to a nameless god hanging at her side. There's a power and a fearfulness to her; there's something in her that's gone a little unknowable, that's taken on the aura of some ancient hierophant or high priestess. She's wearing her coat again. It changes her; changes her posture, broadens her, obscures enough of her body to almost obscure the fact that she's a person at all. She's standing in front of us as an envoy for something we can't understand; she's here as a conducting rod for death.

The bog mummy tenses beside me. This is a big moment for her. I want to be able to touch her, then; I want to put an arm around her shoulder, squeeze her against me and tell her it's going to be okay. I want to hold her hand as we walk through the house to the museum space.

But I can't. So I rise, kind of in awe of the woman in front of me, letting the dead woman at my side cling as close to me as she needs to, and I steel myself for the funeral.

8

The congregation is waiting for us in the museum room, already curving around the body like a crescent moon. It seems immensely dark; the lights are on, casting an orange glow over the space, but there's only a faint light coming through the skylight. I realise that the sun must have set.

The veiled case seems very far away from where the seven strangers have arranged themselves. The edges of the black sheet are dancing in the draught from the door, like the frills of a cuttlefish. It looks alive, like it should be swimming around the room. But at the same time, it sucks in the light and the colour from the space around it, looking as elegantly dead as any object possibly could, the blank black of the fabric darker than anything else in the dull space.

I cross the floor, conscious of how loud and echoing my footsteps suddenly seem, and I look up through the skylight. The clouds are beginning to break apart; I can see the night through them. I can't see the moon, but I can tell where it is by the silver light that haloes a thick patch of clouds. It must be bright tonight, if it's shining that strongly. I wouldn't be surprised if it was a full moon.

I meet Rebecca's eye, and she smiles at me and gives a tiny wave. I carefully peel the veil from the glass coffin and bundle it up as best I can. I hold it close to me. I hear a very quiet gasp from somewhere in the congregation, and the silence of the room seems to intensify, so much that I'm conscious of making any noise at all. That's right; these people won't have seen her before. And I'm aware of something else, too: the bog body isn't hovering near me anymore. I can't sense her presence at my side. She's become the body in the glass case again. This is her, for the time being. She's taken her place for the funeral. Just like the congregation.

Morag comes into the room, slowly and heavily, fully dressed but not put together. She's in a fleece and slippers, her hair still a mess. She gives a sombre wave of acknowledgement to the congregation at the other side of the room, but doesn't go to join them yet. She's waiting for someone. I go over to stand by her at the door. I'm still holding the veil like a comfort blanket. It's very soft. I think it might be real silk.

"Here, pet. I'll take that off of you," Morag murmurs next to me. It slips from my hand like water. She still looks exhausted, but I can see something burning in the back of her eyes now that wasn't there before. She breathes in through her nose, very slowly, straightening herself up as she does so. She's here to do what she's always done; she's here to protect the body.

And then Hazel is here with us. There's a new kind of thrill to the silence in the room as soon as she walks in, an electric current that I feel buzzing off the congregation as they shuffle subtly and try not to stare. I feel it coming off of Hazel, too; I feel it so strongly that I'm sure the hairs on my arms and the back of my neck must be standing up. Being next to her feels like how the air feels before a thunderstorm. I sneak a look at her; at her hawk eyes, and her coat collar and the sharp line of her jaw. I've never stood this near to someone who has their own magnetic field before. It's pretty hot.

I see her take her notebook out of her pocket. It's a beautiful, sleek little thing.

"Hazel," Morag says, voice just loud enough for the two of us to hear. "Remember what we agreed. I'll have no worship of any god under my roof. No god is going to touch her; not now, not ever. Do you understand?"

Hazel tenses slightly. But she nods, respectfully.

"None of the spiritual stuff was ever done to fuck you over, Morag. You know that, don't you? None of it was intended as an insult to you. I just want what's best for her. In case I'm right."

She looks up to meet Morag's eye. Morag meets it right back. Neither of them says anything. Hazel breaks eye contact. Then Morag nods, grimly. "In case you're right."

I want to tell them that the colours in the room are extraordinary. That I wish I could paint so that I could go home and make a painting of this exact scene. Instead, I say, "I think I want to film it. Would that be okay?"

Hazel shrugs. Morag's already crossed over to the bog body in her glass coffin.

She stands at the body's right side, her hand resting protectively on the glass. Hazel comes to join her, standing at the head of the coffin, not quite close enough to touch it. I don't need to be told what to do. I take a few steps back so I can get all of it in shot. I turn on my phone and start to record.

I frame them, Hazel in three-quarter view, Morag in profile. I tap the screen so that it brings up a grid over the camera, splitting the image into nine boxes, three rows of three. It's the only thing I know about cinematography: where lines intersect, that's where it's powerful. That's where Hazel's face has to go, where the power is, where two lines cross. A faint white crosshair meeting on the apple of her cheek. .I keep it wide, keep all of it in the frame, just like a painting.

She takes up the notebook again, tips it open using her thumb. I'm too far away to see what's inside, but I catch a glimpse of jagged and messy handwriting, thin black ink covering every inch of the page, and it makes my heart leap. I'm sure I see drawings in there, too. Hazel and Morag both look up. The skylight is a square of silver-black hanging in the air above the coffin. I can just about see the moon; full, just like I thought it would be.

"Before we begin, I'd like to extend my thanks to all of you who made the journey to be with us tonight. Welcome to you all. Welcome to this most unusual of ceremonies, and thank you for the efforts you have gone to in order to ensure this ceremony takes place. Thank you for looking at this long-dead person and seeing her as someone worthy of celebrating. Your compassion and empathy for this young woman is a rare and touching thing."

I film her as she takes a breath, cracks her neck to one side just a little, her gaze flicking down to her notebook.

"She is not a pleasant thing to consider, this woman. She is not a comforting image to hold in one's mind for too long a time. She is abject, she is uncanny; too rotten and decayed for our liking, but too well preserved and too lifelike at the same time. Her contradiction can turn a stomach; it is, after all, built into our culture to turn our faces away from the bodies of the dead, as much out of repulsion as out of respect.

"In preparation for this service, I found myself thinking about the process of decay in the natural world. About the funeral rites that exist within nature. I think of the bodies of sperm whales that sink slowly to the bed of the ocean, and become ecosystems. They sustain life for months and months, for smaller and smaller creatures until their skeletons lie on the ocean floor, stripped bare. In nature, there is no sense of abjection. No boundary marked between life and decay.

Nature simply breaks matter down, and builds new things from it.

"For the longest time, our culture has dithered on the edge of finding this process beautiful, admiring it with a wistful sort of respect, but never venturing so far as to incorporate it into our own mourning. For us, there is no poetry in returning a body to the natural cycle. There is only rot. A dead body is something to be hidden away; the process of decomposition unsightly and dehumanising.

"So now, confronted with the image of a human body in a preserved state of half-decay, we have a choice to make. We can either look away in revulsion, or we can take a moment to appreciate the machinations of the earth that allowed this body to become a part of the land, to have its fats and soft tissues broken down to sustain the bog it was buried in, but also to keep its human shape, to remind that this body was once a person.

"The notion of a thousand years is difficult for us to understand. It's a length of time that stretches out beyond our lifespans to a dizzying distance, past wars and kings and empires. But that's how long this body has lain beneath the bog. This woman was alive a thousand years ago. One thousand years. Somehow, through the intricate processes of the bogland, this woman's body seems to have slipped through a thousand years as if it were nothing.

"Listen—"

She cocks her head to the sound of the whistling through the old, creaking building. And the rain, pattering against the roof.

"Listen to this place. This is how the sky behaves when there's no cities in its way. This is how loud and angry the weather can sound when there's no buildings to soak it up and no noise of people to drown it out. In this weather, in this flat, sprawling land, it starts to feel as if no time has passed between her lifespan and ours. There's nothing to separate us from this woman but the box she's kept in. The smell of bracken and peat is drifting in from the bog, can you smell it? Can you taste it in the back of your throat? Breathe it in. You could walk out of this room into paganism and druidry and wild, ungodly ritual. The brutality that she lived through is not at as comfortable a distance from us as we might like to think.

"If this were a different funeral, I would usually dedicate some time to talking about the deceased person; telling the story of her life, reminding us what she cared about and what she valued, inviting loved ones to share their memories of her. We can't do any of that today. We know nothing of who she was; all we can do is grasp at what clues her body gives us. We know she was undernourished. We know she was strong from a life of hard labour. And we know she was younger than anybody here in this room."

Hazel looks up from her notebook to meet my eye for a fraction of a second.

"We can't tell what kind of a woman she was from her body. But her body tells us how she died. When Morag Ross found this woman in the bog, she found her with a noose around her neck. The archaeologists who examined her and tried to buy her from Morag insisted that she keep the noose in place. Morag chose to cut it off. This young woman was killed, brutally and ritualistically, as punishment for a crime that will forever be a mystery to us. The historians and archaeologists suggest it was most likely a religious transgression, or a transgression against her husband. She was garrotted, and her body was sunk into the bog."

Hazel is silent for a moment. And in that moment, I feel this sudden swell, this stab of grief that comes from nowhere, almost strong enough to make me forget to breathe. It's in my ribs, my sternum, hammering against the bones from the inside. I know how to swallow it down, I know how to make it gone again. I know how. I just need to stop my hand from trembling, to keep filming, to see this through to the end.

They killed her.

"What we need to understand, here, in this place where time seems thin and flexible, is that we are not at a distance from what happened to this woman; this act of violence a thousand years ago has ramifications that reach into our lives today. Acts of violence, like the violence that was done to this woman, behave like the body of a whale sinking to the bed of an ocean; they are sustenance for whatever outlives them. Through centuries of executions, witch trials, honour killings, domestic murders, serial killers, hate crimes, we are left with a culture that glorifies women's violent deaths, and idolises their dead bodies.

"Think of the beautiful dead bodies we see on our screens; those pretty, half-naked corpses, so tragic and silent, all the more beautiful for being dead. Think of the paintings where a woman is lying recumbent, in a state of death-like lethargy so complete that even the look on her face is glazed and vacant like a fresh corpse. The less movement, the less life in her, the more beautiful she is. Take the person out of the body and the body becomes an object, and a beautiful body without a person in it is an object of art. The best thing a woman can be is a dead body.

"They put her in the ground after they killed her, and by some miracle the ground chose to preserve her. And yet they won. It is by her death and not her life that she endures. She exists before us, reduced to a corpse, with all the humanity stripped from her. Something abject, something unsightly, dug from the ground. In death, she has ceased to be a person. She has ceased to be anything more than a body.

"But we are here tonight in defiance of this. We are gathered around the remains of what was once a human being. This body is more than a body, the same way each of us is more than a body. This body once sustained a human being, as ours sustain us. These limbs once carried her, these hands were put to labour, these eyes and ears made her aware of danger; the neurons that sparked in her brain gave her thought, gave her an imagination and a sense of self; the chemicals and hormones produced by the glands in her body gave her impulses, gave her adrenaline, gave her sadness and joy. Let us remember, then, that this body was once more than an empty husk of a thing. This body was a miracle of nature; a complex and intricate organism that manifested a human soul. Let her be mourned for what she was; let her be mourned as a human soul."

Morag nods vigorously, her chin pushed down into the folds of her neck. She's crying hard; her face is scrunched red and shining wet. Part of me wants to turn off my phone and rush over to hug her. But I can't, now. Not while the funeral is still in progress.

The moonlight hits the bridge of Hazel's nose as she lifts her eyes from the notebook. "This is a humanist service. But we respect the religious views of everyone present. We will take a moment now to close our eyes and bow our heads, and share in a moment of silent prayer or reflection." As if to demonstrate, she shuts her eyes and lets her face fall forward.

I look across at Morag, taking the focus of the camera with me without really meaning to. She isn't bowed: she stares defiantly out in front of her, not looking at Hazel, not looking at anything. Her jaw is set, her brow knitted, her face still damp from tears. There's anger in that look: a pure and righteous anger. It's an expression I'd never have thought she'd be capable of.

I turn away, scared suddenly that she might catch me staring. I don't know what I'm expecting to see when I look over at Hazel. Her notebook is shut and clasped in both hands. Her eyes are closed, her head bowed, her face open and peaceful in a way that's almost vulnerable. And her mouth is moving silently along with the words of a personal, secret prayer.

When it's over, I film the congregation as they trail slowly from the museum space, passing by the bog mummy as they go. Each of them glances very deliberately at her as they pass her by. One of them, one of the older women with long silver hair, reaches out and touches the glass of the coffin, then she looks up into my camera like she's been caught doing something she shouldn't be, and follows after the others. Rebecca comes last, and she smiles at me, at the camera, before turning around to take a last look at the bog mummy before she leaves the space.

The only one left in the room with me is Morag, sitting at the far end of the room. She is slumped over, pitched forward slightly like an old drunk. She grips her knees with both hands.

I keep filming her as she sits, holding onto herself with a tender and powerful grip. I frame her, without her knowing, alone against the broad, blank wall, sitting with her grief. I should go over to her; I know I should. But the thing is, that strange swell of grief hasn't gone anywhere. It feels stuck halfway up my throat, like I'm choking on something. Like if I opened my mouth to talk it would block anything from coming out.

So I stop the video and put my phone back in my pocket.

And I just leave.

I find Hazel standing by the open door, leaning on the frame and looking out at the rain. I go out and sit on the step, my feet resting on the rough ground with the grass creeping through the paving, my sleeves pushed up to my elbows.

She watches me as my fingers trace up and down my bare arm. I follow her eyes as she follows my hand. I wonder if she's just going to dissolve into the landscape. If she stands there too long, she'll slowly grow bracken out of the tips of her fingers.

"You know how she stayed so well preserved?" She asks.

"No."

"It's the ground they put her in. If she had been buried in any other kind of soil, she'd be long rotted away. But she was buried here, in the bogland. It had to be the bog, you see, where everything that's required for mummification just happens to naturally converge: the coldness, the acidity, the lack of oxygen. It preserves. It keeps things. Refuses to let them rot."

She doesn't look up from the coffin. Her eyes are glassy, unblinking, stiller than I've ever seen them.

"That's kind of like where I come from, in Ireland. The peat bogs. Did I ever tell you that?"

I shake my head, knowing she can't see.

"When I was a little girl, I would leave my window open every night, even in the winter. I'd go to sleep smelling the peat smoke. And right before I went to sleep, I always had the same thought, that the house could be burning down with me inside, and I'd burn to death thinking the smoke I could smell was the burning peat."

She holds her upturned palm to the corner of her hip. "I had hair down to here when I was a little girl."

I'm looking at her, but not really listening. I'm trying to remember something Ana told me once, about a cinematographer called Jack Cardiff, and that film *Black Narcissus*, which I still haven't seen, and how he lit things in red and green because those colours grate against one another and make everything queasy and unsettled. Green like the landscape, red like the insides of a person when the skin splits open. The bog and the body. I'd said something about Christmas, I'm sure, and it had made her laugh.

This is the door that Hazel broke when we first met. In the moonlight, I can see the spiderwebs that criss-cross it like a cat's cradle. Last night's moon is still lingering faintly through the gaps in the clouds, pale and insubstantial against the grey-blue sky. There's more that I need to say to her than I know how to articulate.

She looks at me. "You didn't know she was killed, did you?"

I realise I'm crying.

Through the blur of the tears in my eyes, she swims into focus. The bog body. I have no other name for her. She sits opposite me, mirroring my posture, my movements. Her shoulders heave as mine heave, her head dipped to match mine, in her own grief and her own shame.

I wonder what she did to deserve death. I wonder if she spoke too loudly and in too much depth about the things she cared about, like Ana did; or vanished into silence for hours on end like me, stretching out the quiet until it made people uncomfortable, because the thoughts in her head couldn't form themselves into words sometimes. I wonder if she hated the feeling of being fucked like I do, every time, even when it's just two fingers; if the feeling of someone else reaching into her body and taking it for themselves made her toes curl like mine do, made her stiffen up like an animal staring down a car, and just lie there and wait for it to be over.

She looks me in the eye and I understand now: she hates being like this. She hates being a dead body and nothing more.

My hand is folded in on itself, middle and ring finger rubbing and scratching the stone in the heel of my thumb, trying to get the pain back, the scrape and rip of ground on skin. It hasn't gone yet, like the sickening presence of the dark cabinet, but it's pushed its way up to the back of my throat, into this compulsion to laugh, or cry, or vomit.

It's raining harder than I think I've ever seen it rain. And I know that isn't right, know that at some point I must have seen it rain like this, seen this much rain fall this heavily out of this grey a sky before, but that's not how it feels. I can't remember seeing anything like it in my life. Neither of us move to close the door, or head back inside.

The rain is making shapes in the middle distance, hitting the wind and the fog and becoming something moving and living, something with form, like twisting pillars in the sky. The sky doesn't know where to end, it's descending to meet us like some god stepping down from heaven to get a look at the damage that's been done. I've gone primal. Time has stopped mattering and I'm only realising now after all these years that the rain is my favourite weather. I love the rain, love it fiercely, angrily, with this deep red painful surge right in my solar plexus that feels like it's trying to burst out of my chest to join in with the rain.

Some animal makes a yelping sound in the distance and I see Hazel cock her head to the noise as if we'd devolved without noticing, pulled back a hundred thousand years of evolution to some ancient state of ourselves; vivid and alert and tuned in to the wild sounds of the night.

I trace my fingers along my forearm, feeling every goosebump under my fingers. I feel oddly detached from it. I'm far away from myself. I've become part of the wilderness.

"I'm so sorry for your loss, Ali."

Then Hazel does something strange. She sits down on the rain-spattered ground, and looks up at me and holds out her arm. Very slowly, making sure I'm not misreading the situation, I sit down beside her. She puts her arm around my shoulders, and pulls me close to her. The ground is soft and wet as I knew it would be. It makes me shiver even more violently. But now her arm is around me and her hand is holding the top of my arm, where the skin is bare, and her warmth is a solid, forceful thing beside me. It levels out the cold. Balances everything into a sort of absence of temperature, a feeling of strange detachment, and yet hyperawareness of every part of me, and every part of her. An absence of anything but the two of us.

"Thank you." That's all I say. There's a lot that I don't say. I don't tell her that sitting there beside her, in the cold and on the rain-spattered ground, I sort of want the ground to grow over both of us and for us to be preserved like bog mummies forever, me leant against her, her against me, her arm locking us together like a hook through an eye.

I press my fingers against the grit in my palm and push it as deep into the flesh as it can go, until the pain is a vague and ghostly throbbing that seems like it's outside my body, or is nowhere at all. I scrunch it up into a fist and release it. It burns and intensifies then washes out like water tipped onto the ground. And something comes unstoppered. Intense and physical, hammering its way from my stomach up to my throat. I feel myself buckling in every rigid place. The bolts holding my body together have come undone. I am racked and racked with painful crying; again and again and again, like waves breaking on stone.

A thousand years ago they murdered a young woman where we're sitting now. They weighed up her transgressions, and decided she had to die. She simply could not be allowed to live. But what they did, here, to that young woman, it didn't break down and dissolve away to nothing in the earth. It stayed preserved. It laid a foundation. A layer of earth for the next layer of earth to be built on. None of it's gone.

Ana died by the same hand that put the bog mummy to death. She was pushed off the edge of the world by the same blunt force, a thousand years later. And I did nothing to stop it. I did nothing to counteract the crushing, grinding pressure of a world built on dead women buried in the ground, and I am going to carry that for the rest of my life. There's nothing that any funeral, any memorial, any act of remembrance can do about it. This sadness that will pollute every memory I have of her. The guilt and the grief will be lurking in my love for her for as long as I'm alive. The dark empty pit cut into the world.

Shaking from the force of it, I lean my forehead against Hazel's shoulder. The wind is so strong and so cold I have to fold in on myself, and into her. Her arm around me is steadying me, holding me to something solid, stopping me from dissolving into the rain.

I look up, squinting against the spitting rain. And there, in the shapes that the rain is making in the dancing wind, I see the bog mummy, tall as a house, standing on the horizon like a great wicker man, towering over us, become something powerful. Become her own god.

"Hazel ... "

"I see her."

9

The early light is low and yellow across the Moss when I get ready to leave the next morning, and I feel its tug again, in that soft part of me that's still moved by all of this. There's something in the way light shines through green. That seems to be all it takes.

Rebecca stayed this time, too. I don't know why. But I find her there in the morning, bleary-eyed and a little dazed. She offers me a lift into Stirling to get my train, and in return I help her load stuff into her car. Turns out she was the one who brought plates, cutlery, Tupperwares full of food, even the tablecloth I'd seen in the kitchen. When I ask her about it, she blushes and says that they'd planned to have a picnic.

I don't get to say goodbye to Morag. My train leaves too early in the morning, and she needs her rest. But as I look up from Rebecca's boot, I see Hazel waiting for me by the door. Her hair is down, somehow making her look more androgynous, like a Viking, or a musician from the nineties.

I go up to her, and there's a moment where neither of us knows what to do, or we both do but nobody wants to move first. Then I hug her. She pulls me in so that my cheek rests on the harsh wool of her coat, while the tip of my nose brushes against her hair. Her hand grips my back tightly. I have my arms around her waist; I feel her slightness, and it feels like only realising how small an animal is when you hold it in your hands. Her coat smells faintly of peat smoke.

"I'm going to come back here," I say, into her shoulder.

"I'll be here when you do."

"Do you think it worked?" I ask Rebecca in her car. "Do you think she's at rest now?"

She doesn't answer right away.

"I don't know," she says. "I don't know how much of that stuff I actually believe in. It's like ... So, I grew up in a Christian house; not crazily so, just like church on Easter and Christmas and when my grandparents were in town, kind of thing. And there's this kind of resentment towards all that religious stuff you get from that kind of upbringing. Because, I mean, I grew up feeling that resentment directed towards me, from the church. As a queer person, as a trans person, but also just like, as a woman, you know?" She meets my eye in the mirror for a second. "But I think it gets under your skin. Even just the... the need for *ceremony*. My mum," Rebecca smiles, watching the road, "my mum talks about *the bells and the smells*. So maybe it's that. Maybe it just feels right to me that she should get a little ceremony."

There's another little silence. "And I liked what Hazel said about her being more than a body," she says after a while. "I liked that a lot. So who knows? Yeah, let's say yes. Let's say that's her at rest, now."

And I know then that Rebecca is wrong. I know that she's here with me, here in the car between us, not quite ready to go.

———

When I get home, I spend a long time staring at my computer screen, looking at the parts of Ana that are left behind on the internet. It doesn't feel destructive anymore; there's no anger in reading what people have said about her. They're trivial, and saccharine, and occasionally so flippant it smarts a little. But there's no malice in them. There's nothing in this outpouring of grief that's any less genuine than a funeral.

I spend the rest of the day looking at the video I made of the ceremony. It looks good. I have a pretty decent camera on my phone; I've never noticed that before. The colours are there, how they were, how I wanted them to be. All the deep oranges of the strip lights above the coffin, and the strange otherworldly glimmering of the faint moonlight through the skylight. There's a blueness to it all as well, like a backdrop, like someone's taken the widest brush you can buy and smeared a midnight blue across the back of the shot in place of the darkness.

I can hear every word that Hazel says. There's a dull, pounding little ache in my breastbone, watching her now. It feels distant from me, and powerful; like fiction, like mythology. Then there's the footage at the very end, of the congregation leaving, of the woman whose name I've forgotten touching the glass of the coffin. And the footage of Morag alone gripping onto her own knees as if they're the only thing anchoring her to the world.

When I edit it all together, the film is about ten minutes long. I have a crick in my back. I'm shuddery and unstable from caffeine and no food. I watch it back, over and over, letting it loop and repeat itself until I know every word and every image by heart.

I go back to my life. I clean my room; I hoover the crawling things out of the carpet, and spray it with a gentle poison to stop them coming back. I keep going to work. I talk to Sarah as if nothing has changed; she doesn't ask me about what I did that one weekend where I disappeared for two nights, and I try not to think of snakes and feel sad when I talk to her.

The difference is that everywhere I go, every minute of every day, the bog mummy is here with me. It's like being the parent of a nervous child; she clings to me, she doesn't want to be out of my sight. When I go to sleep she makes herself small so that she fits under the covers of my single bed next to me. I want to tell Hazel that it hasn't worked. I want her to know that she hasn't been laid to rest.

But I haven't heard anything from Hazel, not even after I sent her the video. I know she's received it, because I got a couple of kind emails from Rebecca and some other members of the congregation, so she must have been able to press the forward button at least. I know she struggles with emails. But she knows how to call me now.

In the end it's Rebecca, not Hazel, who gets in touch to tell me that Morag has died.

I get the email just as I'm about to go to bed. *I'm sorry to tell you this way,* it says. *I know neither of us knew her for that long, but she made such an impact, didn't she? I'm in bits today, Ali. She seemed like the kind of person who'd just keep on going forever.*

The bog mummy is next to me as I read it. And I don't want to disturb her.

It hits me a day later in the last light of a weekday evening, with dust and light spilling into the kitchen through the gaps between the blinds. I'm doing the dishes, the dishwater splashing up my arms and dripping into the rubber gloves, running down my wrists and dampening the ends of my sweatshirt sleeves. And it hits me.

I have to brace myself on the sink. It pours out of me like rain, all of it at once. I still have my rubber gloves on. I wipe my eyes with the space of bare skin between the glove and my sleeve. Again and again, like windscreen wipers. I just stand there. I just cry.

Sarah's there. She hears me crying and comes in, almost, to the kitchen, pausing at the door frame. She hangs there awkwardly, her mouth half open as if she knows there's something she's supposed to say, wanting me to stop, to wipe my eyes and laugh and say I'm fine. But I just look at her. The crying doesn't stop coming. I'm trembling and dripping like I've just been caught in a thunderstorm. I don't want to stop. She's stood there like a frightened animal that's waiting for its moment to bolt, trapped in the doorway by obligation to her friend but prickling with fight-or-flight response.

The bog mummy watches her, not knowing what to do either.

Sarah hugs me back when I hug her, with that firmness and softness that makes hating her impossible. I turn my head into her shoulder, and breathe her in, the soft metallic flower smell of her. She doesn't let go.

She doesn't ask me what's wrong, or try to understand. But she doesn't let go.

I know she won't talk to me about it. But maybe one day, someone will.

That evening, she catches me in the hall before I leave to do what needs done that night. She hovers by the coat rack, absent-mindedly playing with the limp, hanging sleeve of my raincoat.

"Is it bad that I didn't ever ask you why you were into it?"

I stop what I'm doing, sitting on the stairs with my boot halfway on. "You mean the celebrant stuff?"

She shrugs. "I don't get it. I didn't want to say anything, but I don't get it. I don't like asking you things like that because you just go all quiet and dodge the question, and it makes me feel like you're annoyed at me for wanting to know. And it's fine, honestly, I know you're not someone who shares a lot of themselves, and that's okay. But just ... out of all the things you could be, all the careers you could go into. I never understood it. Even for you, that's ... I just never understood."

I stare at nothing for a minute, slowly pulling at my bootlaces as I try to find an answer for her. When I tell her, I'm not even sure if it's the right answer. "I missed Ana's funeral."

She laughs, a one-syllable, knee-jerk response laugh, that barely makes a sound and doesn't change a muscle on her tense, bemused face. The bog mummy gives her a look.

"I didn't really know how to, like ... how to grieve, I suppose." She stands for a minute not knowing what to say. "I didn't know what I was supposed to do. She, uh ... she was pretty much the only person I felt I was the same as, for a really long time. And I don't just mean ... look, you've probably known for a while that I'm not straight or whatever, that I'm not really into boys, and I don't really know how to feel about my body, and I don't really know what the right words are for it yet. But I knew that whatever she was, I was that too. You know? And she took part of with her when she died, and I'm not sure if I'm ever going to get that back."

"Oh, Ali ... " The shape of the smile is still on her mouth but the rest of her face is twisted strangely, pained and tired and so afraid for me, and trying so hard to be kind. Women are kind. Not all of them. But enough of them. Even the ones that seem to find it all so effortless, even down to smelling like they're supposed to. They do the work to be kind.

I stand up, and give her a quick one-armed hug as I'm reaching past her to get my jacket. "I have to go now. I have a thing I want to do."

She doesn't say anything else.

I go back to the grounds of my primary school at that strange time of the night when there's still lights on in people's homes but no movement on the streets.

There's no pitch anymore, of course. The school grounds stop abruptly with a wooden fence, and then it's a new estate of pebbledash houses.

But one of those old floodlights is still there, the same pale, weathered pink light, shining on nothing. It looks old, as if it's been there for generations. The pink light changes the colour of the paving stones and the grass it shines onto; brings out the red in things.

There's a patch of dirt and spattered grass at the space between the path and the new, unwelcome fence. I can see the root of a tree bulging just a little out of the earth. I sit down beside it.

The smell of this place. The shapes the lights throw. It's almost too much, for a moment. And yet I want more. I want the tall wooden fence along the side of the playground to open up like the gates of Saint Peter and the pitch to still be there. I want it the same as it is in my memory, in my child's memory, vast and red like a bloody sea. I want the violence of it, and the dirtiness, and the exhilarating unhappiness of being a child. And in the middle of it, I want my friend. I want to curl up in the gritty, sap-sticky root of a tree with Ana; I want to love her, and lie there forever.

The light reddens the dirt at the side of the path, changing it as it illuminates it, disguising its real colour, or maybe revealing it. There's a tree still here that I remember; not our tree, not the tree that I would have wanted, but it feels like something.

I sit in the dirt, next to the old root of the tree, my hands touching the ground where there's still traces of red gravel. Maybe I should have stayed in Morag's house at the edge of the world. Maybe the only way to win is not to play. Shrug off everything I've spent so long trying to be; burn all my bridges down and breathe in the peat smoke like it was a house on fire.

I open out my hand. The uneven ground has left imprints in my palm, little flecks of dirt pushing into my soft skin. I brush off the dirt, but the marks stay there. I don't know what to do. None of it matters. All of this happened and none of it mattered for anything. The bog mummy's still here.

For a heartbeat, I want Hazel to be here with me. I want her so badly, for a heartbeat, that it makes my throat seize. She'll be the one to officiate Morag's funeral, of course. And I'll be there. I'll be there in whatever way she needs me to be; by her side, watching her from the congregation. It might mark the end of my career as a celebrant, and it might mark the beginning of it. It doesn't matter, now. I want to be there, for Hazel and for Morag.

I wonder what she's going to do with herself, after Morag. But it's meaningless to wonder. I know exactly where she is. I know there's only one place she could possibly be, one duty that she could ever have taken on.

And I think then that if I ever pray to anyone in my life, if I ever feel powerless or hopeless enough or the mood just takes me one day, that's who I'll pray to. Not to any god, or any metaphysical power, but to Hazel Weir, all alone in the grave-ridden bog, guarding the bog mummy like a sentinel.

And then, squeezing the thought of her hard before letting it go, I put her out of my mind. I put them both out of my mind, for now.

And I think of Ana instead.

This is the first place she and I had together. If our friendship, if our love was preserved in the ground anywhere, it would be preserved here.

In the pink gloom the bog mummy shifts herself into my peripheral vision. The frail little bones of her ribcage expand and contract as she stands there, just hovering; awkwardly, unpleasantly. Why unpleasantly? I'm not repulsed by her anymore. But there's something about her that feels wrong now, something in the way that her face is, in the way the features that would have distinguished her have rotted away, leaving a bland skeleton face that could belong to anyone. There's something offensively impersonal about it. Something vague and noncommittal.

I look at her. Straight on this time, not out of the corner of my eye. In this perfect light she seems cheap and unconvincing, some prop from a horror film, not a person, not even a body; just a *thing*. I'm frustrated at her, suddenly; at her meek expressionless face, her languid body, her placidness, at how easy it was to manipulate her into whatever I wanted her to be. It's not good enough. It's never been good enough. Because there was nothing she was ever going to be but a stand-in. Something easier to swallow than what was really there. As much as I was convinced otherwise, it had never been the bog mummy that was haunting me. All this time, it had always been Ana.

And suddenly, painfully, she is there with me, as she always has been. Ana. My first person. The best of people. She's there with the pink light in her hair, and the moonlight haloing the clouds above her head, in her purest, most savage form, uncorrupted and uncomplicated, as large and as powerful and feral as she should always have been. I see her younger selves shining through her from the inside, nestled in her body like Russian dolls, curled up safe inside one another, protected from harm.

I can't do what Hazel does. I was never meant for this. I don't have it in me to distance myself from it; to be grand and insightful, to make it all into symbolism and words. So this is my funeral. This place, taking her back here and setting her free in the place where my connection to her is the most powerful, like where ley lines meet and mark the touching point of two realities. This is the ceremony; this is me scattering ashes that I don't have in a place that doesn't exist anymore. It won't take the guilt away, and it won't take the pain away, but it's a goodbye. It's a laying to rest.

I close my eyes for a moment against the gentle pink light. Like closing a book. I open them again and look out over the cracked concrete path and the fenced-up playground. I feel very alone, the same way that I was when I stepped off the train up into the Moss. Like an astronaut lost in space.

I don't regret missing her funeral. I don't regret not seeing her body. To reduce someone like that to a body is unthinkable. She will always be more than a body. So that means I'm more than my body, too. But I'm not like Hazel; I don't think I believe in an immortal soul, or a god that takes people's hands as payment. So my body is all I am. I am chemicals in my own brain. I am electricity firing between neurons. We're the same thing; Ana, the bog mummy and me, separated only by some arbitrary spark of life. Theirs has gone out, mine still flickers. For now. The thought should scare me, but instead it sort of warms me, makes me feel something almost like kinship.

I look up at the sky, and for a moment I'm lying in the roots of the trees by the red pitch with Ana by my side, her hair catching the pink lamplight. She's there with me.

I watch the moon illuminate the clouds from behind, until it slowly comes into view; waning now, but bright enough to bring out the colours in things, while the stars that have made it through the light pollution flicker overhead.

I keep staring for a long time, because I know that Ana will be gone when I look back.

ACKNOWLEDGEMENTS

My thanks to Antonia Rachel Ward of Ghost Orchid Press, for your faith in this book.

Thank you to everyone from the M.Phil. programme at Trinity College; in particular to Deirdre Madden and Ian Sansom, for your guidance and wisdom. Thank you to my workshop group, Catherine, Dasom, Kate, Arthur and Nicky, who saw this project come to life in real time, for better or worse. Thank you to *Misplacement Magazine* for publishing an excerpt from an early draft.

Thank you to all my friends who volunteered to read some version of this over the years: Alyson, Gemma, Supriya, Elizabeth, Micaela, Rowan, Matt, Louise, and both Madeleines. My love and gratitude, as always to Margaret, David and Marcus Allan.

And thank you, last of all, to the bog bodies on display in the National Museum of Ireland.

ABOUT THE AUTHOR

Lucy Elizabeth Allan was born in Glasgow. She has a Master's in creative writing from Trinity College Dublin, and is studying towards a PhD at the University of Glasgow. *Skin Grows Over* is her first novella.

ALSO AVAILABLE
FROM GHOST ORCHID PRESS

GHOSTORCHIDPRESS.COM